PENGUIN CLASSICS

Maigret and the Informe

'I love reading Simenon. He makes me think of Chekhov'
– William Faulkner

'A truly wonderful writer . . . marvellously readable – lucid, simple, absolutely in tune with the world he creates'
– Muriel Spark

'Few writers have ever conveyed with such a sure touch, the bleakness of human life'
– A. N. Wilson

'One of the greatest writers of the twentieth century . . . Simenon was unequalled at making us look inside, though the ability was masked by his brilliance at absorbing us obsessively in his stories'
– *Guardian*

'A novelist who entered his fictional world as if he were part of it'
– Peter Ackroyd

'The greatest of all, the most genuine novelist we have had in literature'
– André Gide

'Superb . . . The most addictive of writers . . . A unique teller of tales'
– *Observer*

'The mysteries of the human personality are revealed in all their disconcerting complexity'
– Anita Brookner

'A writer who, more than any other crime novelist, combined a high literary reputation with popular appeal'
– P. D. James

'A supreme writer . . . Unforgettable vividness'
– *Independent*

'Compelling, remorseless, brilliant'
– John Gray

'Extraordinary masterpieces of the twentieth century'
– John Banville

ABOUT THE AUTHOR

Georges Simenon was born on 12 February 1903 in Liège, Belgium, and died in 1989 in Lausanne, Switzerland, where he had lived for the latter part of his life. Between 1931 and 1972 he published seventy-five novels and twenty-eight short stories featuring Inspector Maigret.

Simenon always resisted identifying himself with his famous literary character, but acknowledged that they shared an important characteristic:

> My motto, to the extent that I have one, has been noted often enough, and I've always conformed to it. It's the one I've given to old Maigret, who resembles me in certain points . . . 'understand and judge not'.

Penguin is publishing the entire series of Maigret novels.

GEORGES SIMENON

Maigret and the Informer

Translated by WILLIAM HOBSON

PENGUIN BOOKS

PENGUIN CLASSICS

UK | USA | Canada | Ireland | Australia
India | New Zealand | South Africa

Penguin Books is part of the Penguin Random House group of companies
whose addresses can be found at global.penguinrandomhouse.com.

Penguin
Random House
UK

First published in French as *Maigret et l'indicateur* by Presses de la Cité 1971
This translation first published 2019
002

Set in 12.5/15 pt Dante MT Std
Typeset by Jouve (UK), Milton Keynes
Printed and bound in Great Britain by Clays Ltd, Elcograf S.p.A.

ISBN: 978–0–241–30436–5

www.greenpenguin.co.uk

MIX
Paper from
responsible sources
FSC® C018179

Penguin Random House is committed to a
sustainable future for our business, our readers
and our planet. This book is made from Forest
Stewardship Council® certified paper.

Maigret and the Informer

1.

When the telephone rang, Maigret groaned with annoyance. He hadn't the slightest idea what time it was, and it didn't occur to him to look at the alarm clock. He was emerging from a deep sleep and still felt a tightness in his chest.

He shuffled over to the telephone in bare feet like a sleepwalker.

'Hello.'

He didn't take in that it was his wife, rather than him, who had switched on one of the bedside lights.

'Is that you, chief?'

He didn't recognize the voice immediately.

'It's Lucas here. I'm on the night shift. I've just had a call from the eighteenth arrondissement.'

'And?'

'They've found a man murdered in Avenue Junot.'

That was right at the top of the Butte de Montmartre, not far from Place du Tertre.

'I'm calling because of the dead man's identity. It's Maurice Marcia, who owns La Sardine.'

A distinctively Parisian restaurant on Rue Fontaine.

'What was he doing on Avenue Junot?'

'Apparently he wasn't killed there. First impressions are that he was left there when he was already dead.'

'I'm on my way.'

'Do you want me to send a car to pick you up?'

'Yes.'

Madame Maigret had been watching him from her bed throughout this exchange, but now she got up and felt around for her slippers.

'I'll go and make you a cup of coffee.'

It was a bad night for it – or maybe too good a one. It had been the Maigrets' turn to have the Pardons over for dinner. There was an unspoken agreement between them, consolidated over the years.

Once a month Doctor Pardon and his wife would have the Maigrets over to dinner at their apartment in Boulevard Voltaire. Then two weeks later it would be their turn to come to Boulevard Richard-Lenoir.

The wives would cook up a storm and swap recipes, while the husbands would chat idly over a glass of sloe gin or raspberry brandy.

Tonight's dinner had been a particular success. Madame Maigret had made a pintadeaux en croute, and Maigret had dug out from his cellar one of the last bottles from a case of vintage Châteauneuf du Pape that he had bought at auction one day when he was passing Rue Drouot.

The wine was superb, and the two men hadn't left a drop. How many little glasses of sloe gin had they followed it up with? Either way, when he was jolted awake at two in the morning, Maigret didn't feel his best.

He knew Maurice Marcia well. Everyone in Paris did. Back when he was a duty inspector, before Marcia had become a respectable member of society, he had had him in his office for questioning on various occasions.

Later, he and Madame Maigret had had dinner from time to time at Rue Fontaine, where the cooking was first-rate.

She brought him his cup of coffee when he was almost dressed.

'Is it serious?'

'It could cause a stir.'

'Someone well known?'

'Monsieur Maurice, as everyone calls him. Maurice Marcia, that is.'

'From La Sardine?'

He nodded.

'Has he been murdered?'

'Apparently. I'd better go and have a look.'

He sipped his coffee, filled a pipe, then went and opened the window a little to see what the weather was like. It was still raining; such a fine, slow rain that you could only see it in the haloes of the streetlights.

'Are you taking your raincoat?'

'I won't bother. It's too hot.'

It was only May – a glorious May until recently, but then the weather had broken, and storms had given way to this vague drizzle that had been falling for the past twenty-four hours.

'See you soon.'

'You know, that guinea fowl you made was marvellous.'

'Not too heavy?'

He chose to leave that question unanswered because he could still feel it sitting on his stomach.

A small black car was waiting for him at the door.

'Avenue Junot.'

'What number?'

'You'll probably see a crowd.'

The streets looked black and glossy, as if they had been lacquered. There was almost no traffic. It took only a few minutes to get to Montmartre, but not the Montmartre of nightclubs and tourists. Avenue Junot was on the fringes, so to speak, of all that hustle and bustle, a street mainly lined with villas which artists, who had started on the Butte and remained loyal to it, had commissioned after becoming successful.

They spotted a crowd on the right-hand pavement and, despite the late hour, saw lights on in the windows and people in their night clothes leaning out.

The local chief inspector had already arrived, a shy, thin little man who came rushing up to Maigret.

'I'm glad you're here, detective chief inspector. This is something that really could cause a scandal.'

'Are you sure it's him?'

'Here's his wallet . . .'

He handed him a black crocodile-skin wallet which was empty except for an identity card, a driving licence and a piece of notepaper with a few telephone numbers written on it.

'No money?'

'A big roll of notes – three or four thousand francs, I haven't counted – in his hip pocket.'

'No gun?'

'A Smith and Wesson that hasn't been used recently.'

Maigret went over to the body and had a strange sensation looking down at Monsieur Maurice. He was wearing a dinner-jacket, as he did every evening, and there was a large bloodstain across his shirt-front.

'Any blood on the pavement?'

'No.'

'Who found the body?'

'I did,' a soft voice said behind him.

It was an old man whose white hair formed a halo around his head. Maigret thought he recognized quite a well-known painter but couldn't remember his name.

'I live in the house just opposite. Sometimes I wake up at night and have trouble getting back to sleep . . .'

He was wearing an old raincoat, which he had put on over his pyjamas, and a pair of red slippers.

'When that happens, I go over to the window and look out. Avenue Junot is quiet, deserted. Cars hardly ever come down here. I was surprised to see a black and white shape on the pavement and I went down to have a look. I rang the police station. These men turned up in a car with its siren blaring, and all the windows filled with inquisitive faces.'

There were about twenty people on the street, passers-by and neighbours in night clothes, looking at the body and the little knot of officials. A local doctor explained:

'That's me finished here. He's very much dead, I can assure you. Now it's a matter for the pathologist.'

'I've called him,' announced the chief inspector. 'And I've informed the prosecutor's office.'

An assistant prosecutor was getting out of a car at that

7

moment, in fact, accompanied by his clerk. He was surprised to find Maigret on the scene.

'Do you think it's an important case?'

'I'm afraid it might be. Do you know Maurice Marcia?'

'No.'

'Haven't you ever eaten at La Sardine?'

'No.'

He had to explain to him that it was the sort of place where you were as likely to run into socialites and artists as you were major-league criminals.

Doctor Bourdet, the pathologist who had taken over from Doctor Paul, got out of a taxi, grumbling. He distractedly shook hands and remarked to Maigret:

'Hah! You're here too!'

Bending over the body, he examined the wound by the light of an electric torch produced from his bag.

'Only one bullet, if I'm not mistaken, but large calibre and fired practically at point-blank range.'

'What was the time of death?'

'If he was brought straight here, the murder must have been committed around midnight. Let's say between midnight and one in the morning. I'll tell you more after the post-mortem.'

Maigret went over to Véliard, an inspector from the eighteenth arrondissement who was discreetly keeping his distance.

'Did you know Monsieur Maurice?'

'By reputation and by sight.'

'Did he live locally?'

'I think he lived in the ninth. Around Rue Ballu.'

'He didn't have a mistress around here, did he?'

It was a strange thing to do, really, if you had a dead body on your hands, to travel from another neighbourhood so you could leave it in sleepy Avenue Junot.

'I think I would have heard about it. Someone who could tell you is Inspector Louis of the ninth arrondissement. He knows Pigalle like the back of his hand.'

Maigret shook hands all round and was getting into the little black car when a journalist appeared, a tall fellow with unkempt red hair.

'Monsieur Maigret . . .'

'Not now. Talk to the inspector or the chief inspector.'

Turning to his driver, he said, 'Rue Ballu.'

He had automatically hung on to the dead man's identity card. Glancing at it, he added:

'21a.'

It was quite a sprawling town-house, one of several in the street, which had been turned into apartments. Among the brass plates on the right of the door, they saw one with the name of a dentist, referring people to the second floor. On the third floor was a neurologist.

The bell woke the concierge.

'Monsieur Maurice Marcia, please.'

'Monsieur Maurice is never in at this time. Not before four in the morning.'

'What about Madame Marcia?'

'I think she's back. I doubt she'll see you, though. Still, have a try if you think it's worth it. First floor on the left. They've got the whole floor, but the door on the right is blocked up.'

The staircase was broad and thickly carpeted, with walls of yellowish marble. The left-hand door didn't have a nameplate. Maigret rang the bell.

There was silence at first. He rang again and eventually heard footsteps inside. Through the door a woman's voice asked sleepily:

'Who is it?'

'Detective Chief Inspector Maigret.'

'My husband isn't at home. Go and ask at the restaurant, Rue Fontaine.'

'Your husband isn't there either.'

'Have you been there?'

'No. But I know he's not there.'

'Wait a moment while I put something on.'

When she opened the door, she was wearing a golden-yellow dressing gown over a white silk nightdress. She was young, much younger than her husband, who was several years older than Maigret, around sixty or sixty-two.

She observed Maigret indifferently, with the merest flicker of curiosity.

'Why are you looking for my husband at this time of night?'

She was tall and very blonde, with the thin, lithe body of a model or a chorus girl. She couldn't have been more than thirty.

'Come in . . .'

She opened the door to a large drawing room and turned on some lights.

'When did you see your husband last?'

'Around eight, as usual, when he left for Rue Fontaine.'

'In his car?'

'Of course not. It's five hundred metres away.'

'Doesn't he ever take his car?'

'Only when it's pouring with rain.'

'Do you sometimes go with him?'

'No.'

'Why not?'

'Because it's not my place. What would I do there?'

'So, you spend your evenings here, do you?'

She seemed surprised by these questions but didn't take offence. She didn't show much curiosity either.

'Most of them. Like everyone, I sometimes go to the cinema.'

'You don't drop in and say hello when you're passing?'

'No.'

'Did you go to the cinema tonight?'

'No.'

'Did you go out?'

'No. Except to walk the dog. I only stayed out for a few minutes because it was raining.'

'What time, roughly?'

'Eleven? Maybe a little later.'

'You didn't run into anyone you know?'

'No. What's the point of these questions? Why are you interested in what I was doing this evening?'

'Your husband is dead.'

She stared at him, wide-eyed. Her eyes were light blue, rather affecting. She opened her mouth as if to scream, but her throat closed up and she brought her hand to her chest. She searched for a handkerchief in the pocket of her dressing gown, then buried her face in it.

Maigret waited, sitting motionless in an uncomfortable Louis XV armchair.

'His heart?' she asked finally, crumpling the handkerchief into a ball.

'What do you mean?'

'He didn't like to talk about it but he had a heart condition which he saw Professor Jardin about.'

'He didn't die of heart failure. He was murdered.'

'Where?'

'I don't know. His body was moved afterwards to Avenue Junot and dumped on the pavement.'

'That's impossible! He didn't have any enemies.'

'He seems to have had at least one because he was shot.'

She jumped up.

'Where is he now?'

'At the Forensic Institute.'

'You mean they're going to . . .'

'Perform a post-mortem, yes. There's no way around it.'

A little white dog trotted slowly down the corridor and rubbed itself against its mistress's legs. She seemed oblivious.

'What are they saying at the restaurant?'

'I haven't been there yet. What could they say?'

'Why he left La Sardine so early. He's always the last to leave. He locks the door before cashing up.'

'Have you worked there?'

'No. It's just a restaurant. They don't have dance numbers or singing acts.'

'Did you used to be a dancer?'

'Yes.'

'Don't you dance any more?'

'Not since I got married.'

'How long ago was that?'

'Four years.'

'Where did you meet him?'

'At La Sardine . . . I used to dance at the Canary. If we didn't finish too late I'd sometimes go and have something to eat there.'

'Is that when he noticed you?'

'Yes.'

'Were you a hostess too?'

She pulled a face.

'It depends what you mean by that. If a customer asked us, we wouldn't refuse to drink a bottle of champagne with him, but that's as far as it went.'

'Did you have a lover?'

'Why do you ask me that?'

'Because I'm trying to find out who could have a grudge against your husband.'

'Well, I didn't have one when I met him.'

'Was he jealous?'

'Very.'

'Were you?'

'Don't you think, detective chief inspector, this line of questioning is a little distasteful when a woman has just learned of her husband's death?'

'Do you own a car?'

'Maurice recently gave me an Alfa Romeo.'

'What about him? What car did he have?'

'A Bentley.'

'Did he drive?'

'He had a driver, but he did drive himself sometimes.'

'I'm sorry to have been so unpleasant. Unfortunately, it's my job . . .'

He stood up, sighing. The large drawing room, which had a magnificent Chinese carpet in the centre, was perfectly silent.

She showed him to the door.

'I may have further questions in the next couple of days. Would you rather I called you in to Quai des Orfèvres or came to see you here?'

'Here.'

'Thank you.'

She replied with a curt good evening.

His stomach still felt strange and his head was heavy.

'La Sardine, Rue Fontaine.'

A few expensive cars were still parked in front of the restaurant, and a liveried doorman was pacing about on the pavement. Maigret went in and took a breath of cool, air-conditioned air.

A head waiter he knew well, Raoul Comitat, came rushing up.

'A table, Monsieur Maigret?'

'No.'

'If you're after the boss, he's not here.'

The head waiter was bald and sickly looking.

'That's unusual, isn't it?'

'It almost never happens . . .'

The restaurant was spacious, with twenty or twenty-five tables. The beams on the ceiling were exposed, the walls panelled in old oak up to three-quarters of their height. Everything was heavy, opulent, but free of most of the tasteless elements that are invariably part and parcel of the rustic style.

It was after three o'clock. There were only about ten people left, predominantly actors and performers, eating quietly.

'What time did Marcia leave?'

'I couldn't tell you exactly but it must have been around midnight.'

'Didn't that surprise you?'

'It certainly did! I doubt it's happened more than three or four times in twenty years. Besides, you know what he's like. I've served you and your wife a number of times. Always in his dinner-jacket, standing there with his hands behind his back, watching. Looks as if he never moves but he sees everything. You think he's out front and he's already in the kitchen or the office.'

'Did he say he was coming back?'

'He just muttered:

' "See you in a while." '

'We were by the cloakroom. Yvonne handed him his hat. I reminded him it was raining and suggested he take his raincoat, which I could see on a hook.

' "No need. I'm not going far," he said.'

'Did he seem concerned?'

'It was hard to tell from his expression.'

'Angry?'

'Definitely not.'

'Did he get a telephone call just before he left?'

'You'll have to ask at the desk. All the calls go through the cashier. But, tell me, why these questions?'

'Because he's been shot dead, and his body has been found lying on the pavement in Avenue Junot.'

The head waiter's features stiffened and his lower lip started to tremble slightly.

'That can't be,' he muttered to himself. 'Who could have done that? I can't think of a single enemy he had. He was a good man, deep down, very happy, very proud of his success. Was there a fight?'

'No. He was killed somewhere else and then taken, probably by car, to Avenue Junot. You said he was wearing a hat when he went out, didn't you?'

'Yes.'

There had been no sign of a hat on the ground in Avenue Junot.

'I've got a few questions to ask the cashier.'

The head waiter hurried over to a table that was asking for the bill. The bill was ready, and he put it on a plate, half covered with a napkin.

The cashier was a small, slender brunette with beautiful dark eyes.

'I'm Detective Chief Inspector Maigret.'

'I know . . .'

'There's no reason to keep you in the dark any longer: your employer has just been murdered.'

'So that's why you and Raoul looked as if you were plotting . . . I'm stunned . . . He was standing right where you are only moments ago.'

'Did he get any telephone calls?'

'Only one, just before he left.'

'From a man? A woman?'

'That's just what I wondered. It could have been either, a man with a slightly high-pitched voice or a woman with a rather deep one.'

'Had you heard that voice before?'

'No. They asked to speak to Monsieur Maurice.'

'Is that what they called him?'

'Yes. Like all his friends. I asked who was calling and they said:

' "He'll know."

'I looked up, and Monsieur Maurice was already standing there, in front of me.

' "Is it for me? What name did they give?"

' "No name."

'He frowned and reached for the telephone.

' "Who is this?"

'Naturally I couldn't hear what the person on the other end was saying.

' "What's that?" Monsieur Maurice went on, "I can't hear you properly . . . What? . . . Are you sure? . . . If I get my hands on you . . ."

'They must have been calling from a telephone box because they put more money in. I recognized the sound.

' "I know where that is as well as you do . . ."

'He slammed the phone down. He was heading for the

17

door when he swung round and went into his office, behind the kitchens.'

'Does he often go in there?'

'Hardly ever during the evening. When he comes in he goes in there to have a look at the post. In the evenings after we close I take him the money, and we go over it together.'

'Is the money kept here overnight?'

'No. He takes it away in a briefcase, a special one we only really use for that.'

'He would carry a gun as well, I imagine?'

'He takes his automatic out of the drawer and puts it in his pocket.'

Monsieur Maurice hadn't been carrying any money that night but he had still gone back to his office to fetch his gun.

'Is there another gun which is kept here the whole time?'

'No. That's the only one I know of.'

'Will you show me his office?'

'One moment . . .'

She handed a note to Raoul Comitat.

'This way.'

They went along a corridor with green walls. On the left, a glass panel gave a view of the kitchen, where four men seemed to be tidying up.

'Here it is. I suppose you have the right to go in.'

The office was simple, not ostentatious. Three good leather armchairs, a mahogany Empire desk, a safe behind it, and some shelves with a few books and magazines.

'Is there any money in the safe?'

'No. Just the accounts. We don't really need it. It was there when Monsieur Maurice bought the restaurant, and he never had it taken out.'

'Where was the gun usually kept?'

'In the right-hand drawer.'

Maigret opened it. There were papers, cigarettes, cigars, but no automatic.

'Does Madame Marcia often ring her husband?'

'Hardly ever.'

'Did she ring him this evening?'

'No. The call would have come through me.'

'What about him? Doesn't he ring her?'

'Rarely. I can't remember the last time he did. It was sometime before last Christmas.'

'Thank you.'

Maigret was feeling the weight of his tiredness and collapsed on to the back seat of the little black car.

'Boulevard Richard-Lenoir.'

The rain had stopped, but the ground was still glistening, and the sky was clearing in the east.

He had a vague sense that something about all this didn't add up. It was true that Monsieur Marcia was no saint. He had had a pretty turbulent youth and had been convicted of procuring a number of times.

Then he had risen through the ranks when he was about thirty, becoming proprietor of what at the time was one of the most famous brothels in Paris, in Rue de Hanovre.

The brothel wasn't in his name. He spent the better part

of his afternoons at the races and, if not, was generally to be found playing cards with other crooks in a bistro on Rue Victor-Massé.

Some people called him the Judge. They claimed that when there was a dispute between figures in the underworld, he would have the final say.

He was a good-looking man, dressed by the best tailors, never wore anything but silk underwear. He was married and already living on Rue Ballu at that time.

He was growing stouter with age, which gave him added gravitas.

Wait! Maigret had forgotten to ask the cashier if the person who had called had had an accent. That could prove important at some stage.

For the moment, though, he was at a complete loss. He remembered something Maurice Marcia had said during one of their last encounters at Quai des Orfèvres. Marcia hadn't been a suspect himself, but his barman seemed to have been involved in a hold-up of a branch of one of the big banks in Puteaux.

'What do you think of this Freddy?'

The barman was called Freddy Strazzia and came from Piedmont.

'I think he's a good barman.'

'Do you reckon he's honest?'

'Well, inspector, it depends what you mean by that. There's honest and then there's honest. When you and I first met, when we were both what's called cutting our teeth, I didn't think of myself as a dishonest man, an opinion not shared by you or the judges.

'Gradually, I've changed. You could say I've spent almost forty years of my life becoming an honest man. Well, it's like with religious converts. They're meant to be the most devout, aren't they? Similarly, people who have worked to become honest tend to be more scrupulous than other folk.

'You're asking me if Freddy is honest. I wouldn't stake my life on it but what I am certain of is that he's not stupid enough to get himself tangled up in a mess like this.'

The car had stopped in front of his building. He thanked the driver and slowly climbed the stairs, slightly short of breath. He couldn't wait to lie down in bed and close his eyes.

'Tired?'

'I'm exhausted.'

Less than ten minutes later he was asleep.

It was almost eleven when he began to stir, and Madame Maigret immediately brought him a cup of coffee.

'Look at that!' he exclaimed in surprise. 'The sun's back.'

'Was it this case in Rue Fontaine that kept you out last night?'

'How do you know that?'

'The radio. The papers. Monsieur Maurice seems to have been a real Parisian celebrity.'

'Character, I'd say,' he corrected.

'Did you know him?'

'Ever since I started in the Police Judiciaire.'

'Do you understand why they went and dumped his body in Avenue Junot?'

'I don't understand anything so far,' he admitted. 'Least of all the fact that Marcia had his gun in his pocket.'

'So?'

'I'm amazed he didn't fire first. He must have been taken by surprise.'

Putting on his dressing gown, he went and sat in the bedroom armchair, picked up the telephone and dialled the number of the Police Judiciaire.

Lucas, who had been on night duty, would be sleeping peacefully by now. It was Janvier who answered.

'Not too tired, chief?'

'No. I'm all right now. Are you up to date with what's going on?'

'From the papers and the latest reports that have just come in, particularly the one from the eighteenth. I also got a call from Doctor Bourdet.'

'What does he say?'

'The shot was fired from about a metre, possibly a metre and a half. The gun is most likely a short-barrelled revolver, a .32 or .38. He's sent the bullet to the laboratory. As for poor Marcia, his death was almost instantaneous, from an internal haemorrhage.'

'So he didn't bleed much?'

'Hardly at all.'

'Did he have a heart defect?'

'Bourdet didn't say anything about that. Do you want me to ring him?'

'I'll do it. I'll be in early this afternoon. Call me if anything, no matter what, comes up before then.'

A few minutes later he had Doctor Bourdet on the line.

'I suppose you're just getting out of bed,' Bourdet said to Maigret. 'I worked until nine this morning and now they've brought me another customer, a woman this time.'

'Listen, other than the gunshot wound, did you notice anything out of the ordinary, any sign of illness?'

'No. He was a healthy man, in very good shape for his age.'

'Nothing wrong with his heart?'

'As far as I can tell, his heart was in good condition.'

'Thank you, doctor.'

Hadn't Marcia's blonde wife Line mentioned Professor Jardin, who her husband went to see from time to time? He called the professor's office, then the hospital where he was told he was.

'Sorry to disturb you, professor. It's Detective Chief Inspector Maigret here. I think one of your patients met with a violent death last night. Maurice Marcia.'

'The Montmartre restaurant owner?'

'Yes.'

'I only saw him once. I think he was planning to take out life insurance and, before undergoing the official medical, he wanted to see a doctor of his own choosing.'

'What were the results?'

'His heart was in perfect condition.'

'Thank you.'

'Well,' asked Madame Maigret, 'was he ill?'

'No.'

'Why did his wife tell you . . .?'

'Your guess is as good as mine. Would you mind getting me another cup of coffee?'

'What do you want to eat?'

He still remembered his indigestion during the night.

'Ham, boiled potatoes with oil and a green salad.'

'Is that all? Haven't you digested my guinea fowl?'

'I have, yes, but I think Pardon and I overdid it on the sloe gin a little. Not to mention the wine.'

He stood up with a sigh and lit his first pipe of the day, then went and planted himself in front of the open window. He hadn't been there for more than ten minutes before he was summoned to the telephone.

'Hello, chief, Janvier here. I've just had a visit from Inspector Louis of the ninth arrondissement, who was hoping to see you. Apparently, he's got something interesting to tell you. He's wondering if you can see him early this afternoon.'

'Tell him to come to my office at two.'

You never knew with Louis. He was a strange man. About forty-five years old, he had been a widower for roughly fifteen years and yet still dressed in black from head to foot, as if he were as much in mourning for his wife as ever. Among themselves, his colleagues in the ninth called him the Widower.

You never saw him laugh or joke. When he was on desk-duty he worked without a break. Being a non-smoker, he didn't even have to stop to light a pipe or cigarette.

Most of the time he worked out of doors, preferably at night. He probably had the most comprehensive knowledge of Pigalle of anyone in Paris.

He rarely spoke to a prostitute or a pimp without good

reason, and they watched him go by with a certain trepidation.

He lived alone in the apartment he had once shared with his wife, on the other side of the boulevard, at the bottom of Rue Lepic. He had been born in the neighbourhood himself. People often saw him doing his shopping.

He knew the pedigree of all the local crooks, the life stories of all the girls.

He would go into bars without taking off his hat and invariably order a quarter bottle of Vichy mineral water. He could stay there for a long time, watching. Sometimes he would chat to the barman.

'I didn't know Francis was back from Toulon.'

'Are you sure?'

'He's just spotted me and slipped off to the gents.'

'I didn't see him. I'm surprised because usually he comes and says hello when he's up in Paris.'

'It's probably because of me.'

'Who was he with?'

'Madeleine.'

'That's his old girlfriend.'

He never took notes and yet all the surnames, first names and nicknames of these ladies and gentlemen of the night were carefully filed away in his brain.

Rue Fontaine was in his area. He must have known more about Monsieur Maurice than Maigret or anyone really. Besides, he can't have come to Quai des Orfèvres by chance, because he was a shy man.

He knew that he would never rise above the rank of inspector and quietly accepted this fact, doing his job as best he could. Having no other passions, he dedicated his life to his work.

'I'm going down to buy some ham.'

He watched her through the window as she headed off towards Rue Servan. He was glad to have a wife like her and there was a little smile of satisfaction on his lips.

How long had Inspector Louis lived with his wife before she was run over by a bus? A few years at most, as he was only thirty when it happened. He had been looking out of the window, like Maigret now, and the accident had happened right there in front of him.

Maigret touched wood, not a habit of his, and waited at the window until he saw his wife cross the boulevard again and go back into the building.

Louis was the inspector's surname. For a while Maigret had thought of adding him to his squad, but he was so lugubrious the atmosphere in the inspectors' office would have been affected.

In the office in the ninth arrondissement, which was staffed by only three inspectors and a trainee, they made sure Louis worked outside as much as possible.

'Poor man!'

'Are you talking to yourself?'

'What did I say?'

'You said, "Poor man." Were you thinking about Marcia?'

'No. I was thinking about someone who lost his wife fifteen years ago and still wears mourning.'

'He doesn't dress all in black though, does he? No one does that any more.'

'He does. He doesn't care what people think. Some people think he's a priest when they first see him and call him "Father".'

'Aren't you going to shave? And get ready?'

'Yes. But I'm feeling lazy, it's lovely.'

He finished his pipe before going into the bathroom.

2.

The windows in Maigret's office were open again to the breezes outside and the sound of cars and buses on Pont Saint-Michel.

Inspector Louis was perched on the edge of the chair Maigret had pointed him to. His movements were slow, almost solemn, like his black suit which was even more conspicuous on this spring day.

'Thank you for seeing me, detective chief inspector.'

He had delicate, very white skin, almost like a woman's, which made his thick black moustache stand out. His lips were red, as if he was wearing lipstick, and yet there was nothing remotely effeminate about him.

He must have been the shy one in class, the boy who blushed and stammered when his teacher spoke to him.

'I'd like to ask you something.'

'Please.'

'Does the fact the body was found on Avenue Junot mean the eighteenth's inspectors will be investigating the case?'

Maigret had to think before answering.

'They're certainly going to question potential witnesses, look for the car that stopped on the avenue in the middle of the night, talk to the old painter who called the police and the other neighbours . . .'

'What about everything else?'

'As you know, it's a Crime Squad case. Not that that means we can't accept or request help from inspectors from other arrondissements. You know Montmartre well, don't you?'

'I was born there and I still live there.'

'Have you come into contact with Maurice Marcia?'

'With him and his staff.'

He blushed. He must have been making a great effort to say everything he had come to say.

'You see, I mainly work at night, so I've ended up getting to know everybody. They're used to me in Pigalle. I exchange a few words with this person or that person. I go into the bars and cabarets, where they give me a quarter bottle of Vichy without waiting for me to order anything.'

'I imagine you've come to see me because you've got an idea about Marcia's murder.'

'I think I know who killed him.'

Leaning back in his chair slightly, Maigret took a gentle drag on his pipe and studied the inspector with curiosity, even a certain fascination.

'Do you have anything to back up your suspicions?'

'Yes and no.'

He was embarrassed and didn't dare look Maigret in the face.

'I got a call this morning.'

'Anonymous?'

'More or less. I've been getting calls from the same person for years.'

'A man or a woman?'

'A man. He's always refused to tell me his name. Whenever something at all mysterious happens in Montmartre he calls me and always starts by saying: "It's me."

'I recognize his voice. I know he is calling from a telephone box and he doesn't waste any time, just tells me the essentials. For instance:

' "They're planning an armed robbery in La Chapelle. It's Coglia's gang." '

'Coglia's still got another few years in prison,' Maigret objected.

'His old accomplices are still at it.'

'Does your informer ever get it wrong?'

'No.'

'Does he ask you for money?'

'No, he doesn't do that either. Or ask me to turn a blind eye to any more or less illegal activities.'

Maigret was growing interested.

'And he called you this morning, did he?'

'Yes. At eight o'clock, which is just before I go out and do my shopping. I live on my own and have to do my shopping myself.'

'What did he say exactly?'

' "Monsieur Maurice has been shot by one of the Mori brothers." '

'Is that all?'

'That's all. Do you know the Mori brothers, Manuel and Jo?'

'We've been trying to catch them red-handed for more than two years. We haven't managed to pin anything on them yet.'

'I'm watching them too. They don't live together. Manuel, the older brother, who's thirty-two, has a smart, even luxurious apartment on Square La Bruyère.'

Just around the corner from La Sardine.

'Jo, who's twenty-nine, has a suite at the Hôtel des Iles in Avenue Trudaine . . .

'But you must have all this information in their file. They have a wholesale fruit and vegetable business on Rue du Caire. One or other of them is there every day. It's a long warehouse which you walk into off the street.'

'Were they in touch with Monsieur Maurice?'

'They'd sometimes go and have dinner at his restaurant. They're not the only crooks who go to La Sardine.'

'Did Marcia ever give them a hand?'

'I don't think so. He'd become cautious and set great store by his respectability.'

'Which of the two brothers was your anonymous caller talking about?'

'I've no idea but I'm sure it won't be long before I get another call. That's why I asked to see you.'

'Do you want to work on the investigation?'

'I want to help somehow, unofficially, in my own way. I've never done anything outside my normal work. You can trust me. I promise I'll keep you informed of anything I find out.'

'Do you know the Mori brothers well?'

'I go to some of the same bars as them. Manuel used to have a Martinican mistress who was very beautiful.'

'What's happened to her?'

'She sings and dances in a club for tourists.'

'Who did he replace her with?'

'No one. Whenever I see him he's on his own or with his brother. The brother lives with a young girl from the country. She's called Marcelle and is twenty-two.'

'Do you think she could be the weak link?'

'She's crazy about Jo Mori and she's got a strong character.'

'Do you think she knows what the two brothers are up to?'

'I don't know how much they trust her. I've never seen them with anyone resembling an accomplice either.'

There had been as many as ten robberies, all done in the same way, using identical techniques. It was always a chateau or large estate in the country within a radius of about 150 kilometres of Paris.

The burglars were well informed. They knew what was of value in the house: objects, paintings, furniture. They also knew if the owners were away and how many people were guarding the property.

They worked silently, without excessive force. Whatever could be sold with relative ease would be moved out in less than an hour, suggesting they had at least one lorry.

Well, the Mori brothers had two of those for their fruit business. And coincidentally enough, they had also started up as wholesalers two years earlier. Before then, Manuel had worked for a buyer in Les Halles, and Jo had spent three years in an architect's office.

Where were the proceeds of the robberies stored? Probably near Paris, in a villa or a house rented under another name.

'Who could have kept an eye on the goods?'

'I can't swear to it, but I've got a pretty good idea. The Moris' mother.'

'Do you know her?'

'I've never seen her. I know she exists, though. She used to live in Arles with her children. When the sons came up to Paris, she stayed down south for another few years with her daughter, who's married now and lives in Marseille.'

Inspector Louis had been patiently working alone like this for a long time, without the complications of working through official police channels.

'How do you know all this?'

'I watch. I listen. I have contacts in different places, people I do the odd favour for.'

'What's happened to the Moris' mother?'

'She sold her house in Arles with all the furniture and hasn't been seen since.'

'I bet you've searched the countryside around Paris.'

'Occasionally, on Sundays or my days off.'

'Have you found anything?'

'Not yet.'

He blushed again, as if ashamed of his self-confidence.

'What do you know about Madame Marcia?'

'Do you mean the current one? Because there was one before her, who he lived with for almost twenty years. They were a very close couple. It's true he picked her up on the street, but he turned her into a real lady. When she died of cancer, it hit him very hard, and for several months he wasn't the same man.'

There had been a time, when he was still young, when Maigret had worked on the streets, in the railway stations, the Métro, the department stores. Back then he knew everyone in the Parisian underworld too.

But now he was shut up in an office, and his boss was shocked if he interviewed suspects in their homes or ferreted around outside.

'Where did he find his second wife, Line, the one he was living with?'

'She worked as a dancer at the Tabarin first, then the Canary. I think that's where he met her. Despite her profession, she was discreet, dressed conservatively and never slept with clients, apparently. She's a relatively educated woman.'

'Aren't you going to tell me about her background, where her parents are from, what she studied at school?'

Inspector Louis blushed again.

'She was born in Brussels, where her father works in a bank. She went to school until she was eighteen, then followed him into the bank. She came up to Paris with a young man, a painter, who dreamed of making his fortune here. Success did not come as quickly as he had hoped. Line started working in a shop on the Grands Boulevards as a salesgirl.

'The painter dumped her and she ended up at the Tabarin, where she had a walk-on part at first.'

Maigret had known the inspector for years, although it was true their paths rarely crossed and they had little contact with each other. He had considered him a humourless idiot for a while before realizing that actually he was a clever man.

Now he stared at him almost in disbelief.

'Are there many people in Montmartre you're this well informed about?'

'You know, it builds up over the years.'

'Do you keep files?'

'No. It's all in my head. I don't have anything else to do, no other interests in life.'

Maigret stood up and went and opened the door of the inspectors' office.

'Will you come in for a minute, Janvier?'

When Janvier appeared, he said to both men:

'I suppose you know each other?'

They shook hands.

'Inspector Louis and I have just been having quite a long chat about Marcia's murder. Any news on that front?'

'Only that a red car stopped halfway along Avenue Junot for a minute around one in the morning.'

'Our men are pursuing the investigation, of course. But Inspector Louis, who knows some of the people involved, will work on his own and keep us up to date with whatever he discovers. Do you know the Mori brothers?'

'We suspected them for a while of being heads of what's known as the chateau gang.'

'Are they still being watched?'

'Not particularly. We just keep track of them if they leave town. Jo, the younger brother, goes to Cavaillon and the surrounding area fairly often to look for early fruit and vegetables.'

'From now on you're going to set up a twenty-four-hour tail.'

'On both of them?'

'On both of them.'

'Still the chateau business?'

'No. This time it's murder. Maurice Marcia's.'

Janvier automatically looked at his colleague from the ninth. He was clearly not best pleased at Inspector Louis' involvement in the case.

'Does anyone else need watching?'

'The widow.'

'Do you think . . .?'

'I don't think anything, you know that. I'm looking. We're all looking.'

He shook Inspector Louis' hand.

'Are you going back to Montmartre?'

'Yes.'

'Do you have a car?'

'No.'

'I'm going there too. Hop in mine. I'd like you to come with me, Janvier.'

Janvier took the wheel, and Maigret smoked his pipe in the passenger seat next to him, which left Louis alone in the back, not feeling particularly relaxed.

He had always dreamed of working directly for Quai des Orfèvres so the mission Maigret had given him was like a promotion.

When they got to Rue Notre-Dame-de-Lorette, Janvier asked:

'Where are we going?'

'Further up. Rue Ballu.'

'To Maurice Marcia's?'

'Yes.'

'Where shall we drop you?'

'Anywhere you like, now I'm on home turf.'

'In that case I'll let you out here.'

'You know how to get hold of me. My home number's in the book.'

'Thank you.'

He got out of the car awkwardly, then set off down the pavement at a steady, unhurried pace.

Moments later, Maigret and Janvier rang the doorbell of the former town-house. The concierge let them in. She was barely forty and rather pretty. She looked at them through the glass door of the lodge until Maigret pushed it open.

'Have they brought the body back?'

'I don't think so, but the undertakers' men are upstairs. I think the body will be here by the end of the afternoon.'

'This is Inspector Janvier, who's also working on the case. How long has Madame Marcia been living in this building?'

'Since they got married. It must be four years.'

'Did they entertain much?'

'Hardly at all. As you know, he never came in before three or four in the morning. He would sleep all morning, have lunch, take a siesta, and then his masseur would come for his appointment.'

'Did he have dinner here?'

'Very rarely. Most of the time he ate at the restaurant.'

'With his wife?'

'No. I don't think he liked her setting foot in La Sardine.'

'Why not?'

'I suppose because he was afraid of who she'd meet. Don't forget that he was in his sixties, and she's barely thirty.'

'What did she do during the day?'

'She gave orders to the cook and the maid. Sometimes she'd go to Fauchon's or some other luxury shop like that to buy things you can't find around here. Once or twice a week she went to the hairdresser's.'

'In town?'

'Rue de Castiglione, I think.'

'And in the evenings?'

'She read or watched television. She'd take her dog out for ten minutes or so before she went to bed.'

'Didn't she go to the cinema?'

'Probably. Once or twice a week she'd be out all evening.'

'Didn't she ever have visitors?'

'Never.'

'Thank you. Is she upstairs?'

'Yes. With her dressmaker.'

They didn't take the lift and rang the bell on the first floor. A young maid with enormous breasts opened the door.

'May I help you?'

'We're here to see Madame Marcia.'

'Madame Marcia is busy.'

'We'll wait.'

'Who shall I say it is?'

'Police Judiciaire.'

'One moment.'

She left them in the entrance and headed to a door at the end of the hall. The drawing-room door was open. The Louis XV furniture had disappeared, as had the big Chinese carpet, and there were some men perched on ladders fixing black hangings on the walls.

So they were doing things on a grand scale, and the drawing room was being turned into a chapel of rest. Presumably that meant the dressmaker was there about the mourning clothes.

'If you'd like to follow me . . .'

She showed them into a study or library lined with books from floor to ceiling. They were leather-bound volumes which Monsieur Maurice had certainly never read.

The armchairs were comfortable. There was a little bar, which must have contained a refrigerator, and the desk, which had red fittings, had nothing on it.

They had chosen the English style for this room. An ivory-inlaid mahogany humidifier was no doubt stocked with expensive Havana cigars. Had these furnishings and things already been here when Line moved in? Or had she added a certain style to the apartment?

'A study where not much work went on,' Maigret muttered to Janvier. 'You should have seen the furniture in the drawing room, it was like being in a museum.

'It will make an impressive chapel of rest.'

Footsteps approached and they fell silent.

She was wearing a black matt-silk dress, very simple,

and a diamond ring which probably never left her finger. She stopped for a moment in the doorway, a look of surprise on her face. Her gaze travelled from Maigret to Janvier. Was she surprised to be confronted by two policemen rather than one? How was she taking it? Did it make their interview seem more official?

'Inspector Janvier, one of the people I work with most.'

She nodded slightly.

'You must realize that I am very busy.'

'We are too, believe me. We're not taking up your time for our own amusement.'

All three of them were standing. As she made no move to, Maigret suggested they sit down.

'Will this take long?'

'I don't think so.'

'You could have asked me anything you wanted to yesterday. I answered you truthfully. The body will be here at seven this evening.'

Maigret pretended not to have heard. Looking around him with an appreciative air, he asked:

'Did the apartment have this furniture when you moved in four years ago?'

'Five,' she corrected him. 'We were a few days away from being married for five years.'

'The furniture?'

'It was bought then. There had been other furnishings before.'

'Not so luxurious, I suppose?'

'In a different style.'

'Whose idea was it to change everything?'

'My husband's. He didn't want to see me living in what had always been his first wife's world.'

'I won't ask if they're genuine. I admired the furniture in the drawing room yesterday . . .'

'They are,' she said grudgingly.

'Did you go with him to buy them?'

'He liked going to antique dealers on his own to surprise me. But I don't see what the furniture . . .'

'It probably has nothing to do with the death of your husband, but we know from experience that you can't overlook anything in a murder case. Was your husband very rich?'

'I didn't discuss money with him. I only know that his restaurant was very successful and that he went to a lot of trouble to ensure it stayed that way.'

'He was very much in love . . .'

'What makes you say that?'

'You don't decorate an apartment like this for a woman you're indifferent to.'

'He loved me.'

'I imagine you married under the convention of common assets.'

'That's normal, isn't it?'

'When is the funeral?'

'The day after tomorrow, at the church of Notre-Dame-de-Lorette. After the service the body will be taken to Bandol, where we have a villa, and he will be buried in the cemetery there.'

'Are you going to Bandol?'

'Of course.'

'Will friends be going?'

'No. I don't know. It's not up to me.'

'Another question. What's going to happen to the restaurant?'

'It's staying open. Apart from the day after tomorrow, the day of the funeral.'

'Who's going to run it?'

She hesitated for a moment.

'I am,' she said eventually.

'Do you think you have enough experience?'

'The staff has worked with my husband for so long it could run itself.'

'Your way of life will change completely.'

Maigret knew she was exasperated by these apparently meaningless questions but he stolidly pressed on.

'My way of life doesn't concern anyone so long as I'm not breaking the law, does it?'

'It was just a thought. You've been living almost like a recluse here. You spend all your evenings alone.'

'No one's stopping me going out.'

'I know. You sometimes go to the cinema. But you don't have any friends, male or female.'

The maid entered tentatively.

'The gentlemen are asking if we have any plants because the room looks bare . . .'

'Show them the ones on the terrace.'

Turning to Maigret, she said:

'You see that I'm needed. Your insistence comes as an unpleasant surprise, especially if you have any sympathy for my husband, as you implied yesterday.'

'I will try to disturb you as little as possible.'

'I must warn you that I've decided not to entertain any more visits from you.'

'I'm sorry to hear that, because in that case I'll have to summon you to Quai des Orfèvres. Your husband often came there in the old days, before he became the owner of La Sardine. He didn't have a villa in Bandol back then either.'

'Do you have to remind me of that unpleasantness?'

'No. Unlike you, your husband had good friends. I was wondering if you know any of them. He may have had them to stay at his villa in Bandol in the summer. The Mori brothers, for instance . . .'

She may have given a start, but if so, it was far too faint for them to be sure.

'Should I know them?'

'I'm asking you. There are two of them, Manuel and Jo. They have a wholesale business on Rue du Caire.'

'I don't know either of them.'

'They ate fairly regularly at La Sardine.'

'Where I never went.'

'One last question. This is a huge apartment. Are you going to carry on living here on your own?'

'My husband always hoped I would, just as he hoped I would keep the restaurant and the house in Bandol.

' "It will be as if a part of me is still there," he'd say.'

'Was he expecting something like this to happen?'

'Absolutely not.'

'But he carried a gun in his pocket.'

'Only when he was bringing back the takings. Anyone who regularly has to move large sums of money has a gun.'

'Talking of which, when he got here, where did he put the money?'

'In the safe.'

'Which is where?'

'Behind that Delacroix picture there, to the right of the fireplace.'

'Do you know the combination?'

'No. I'll have to call out a specialist, or maybe even the company that makes them.'

'Thank you.'

She stood up, and Maigret could tell she was still tense. She seemed to be going over all the questions he had asked her in her head.

Where did they lead to, in fact? Maigret would have been hard put to say himself. He felt uneasy somehow. There were aspects of this case that he didn't like.

He found himself out on the street again with Janvier. The sun was still high and blazing hot.

'Do you think she knows more than she's saying, chief?'

'I'd put money on it.'

'You mean she's . . . let's say, an accessory?'

'I wouldn't go that far, but the story is definitely murkier than she'd have us believe.'

'Where are we going?'

'Rue Fontaine.'

There were no customers at this time of day, but two of the waiters were laying tables for dinner. Freddy, the barman, was wiping bottles and arranging them on the shelves behind the bar.

Maigret headed towards him.

'Is Comitat here?'

'He's having a rest in the boss's office.'

'Already?'

'What do you mean?'

'Monsieur Maurice's not even buried, and he's already taking things easy.'

'You've got it wrong. Even in Monsieur Maurice's time, Raoul used to have an hour's shuteye in one of the armchairs in the office.'

'Do you know the funeral's the day after tomorrow?'

'I hadn't been told that yet.'

'The restaurant will be shut so all the staff can go.'

'That's usually how it's done, isn't it?'

'Afterwards the body will be buried in Bandol.'

'That doesn't surprise me. The boss was born in a village, I can't remember which one, somewhere between Marseille and Toulon, and he'd close the restaurant for a month every year to go and stay in his villa in Bandol.'

'Aren't you wondering what's going to happen to the restaurant?'

'It's all the same to me. Someone's bound to take it on. It's a goldmine.'

'Well, from now on you'll be working for a woman not a man.'

'You're kidding!'

'Madame Marcia has decided to take over from her husband.'

Freddy made a strange face then remarked, 'Well, it's up to her, isn't it.'

'Do you know her?'

'From when she was at the Tabarin. I worked there for a couple of years before I came here. She was in the chorus.'

'What do you think of her?'

'I haven't had much chance to talk to her. When she came to the bar she'd just order a drink, and that was that. I thought she was pretty stuck-up. We're more used to the friendly type here in Montmartre. Saying that, she was classy, I have to admit. She can't be from the sticks. I wouldn't be surprised if she'd had a good education.'

'Do the Mori brothers still come here for dinner often?'

Freddy saw no harm in that question.

'Off and on. They're not regulars. They have to get up early because of their import business, you know.'

'Are they still friends with the boss?'

'Monsieur Maurice would go and sit at their table for a bit, as he always did with good customers. Sometimes he'd offer them a brandy from his private store.'

'Whereas Madame Marcia never came to the restaurant.'

'Never.'

'Do you know why?'

'I suppose because Monsieur Maurice was jealous. She's a pretty girl, if that's your type. There was an age difference of over thirty years between them.'

He looked towards the back of the room.

'Here's Raoul coming to start his shift.'

The head waiter had spotted them. He came over and shook hands with Maigret, then Janvier.

'Did you come to see me?'

'We thought we'd find you here, but we haven't come

for any particular reason. I was telling Freddy that the funeral is the day after tomorrow at the church of Notre-Dame-de-Lorette.'

'We'll be shut, then. Someone really should have told me earlier. I'm the one carrying the whole restaurant on my shoulders at the moment, after all. I've been here for sixteen years and she . . .'

He stopped, embarrassed. He had probably been about to say 'and she's only been sleeping in his bed for five'.

'Do you know who's taking over from Monsieur Maurice?'

'From the way you ask that question, I can guess. In any case, it crossed my mind yesterday. She is, isn't she?'

'Yes. Do you know her?'

'I've seen her in Bandol. The boss knew I was on the coast one summer and invited me to lunch at his villa. That would be a good place to end your days, I can tell you. It's not very big, nothing showy. But it's the genuine article, really sturdy. I'm from the south myself. I know a bit about old Provençal furniture, and I've hardly ever seen pieces like Monsieur Maurice's.'

He turned to Freddy.

'Haven't you offered these gentlemen a drink yet? What are you having?'

'A beer.'

'Me too,' said Janvier, slightly embarrassed.

Comitat sighed:

'Still, it's going to be strange having a woman as boss. Honestly, it'll be like a brothel!'

'I'm sure some of the customers will feel at home.'

'All kinds of people come here, you know. Ministers, artists, directors, even bankers. Lawyers too, and doctors, not to mention, as you just said, a few ex-crooks.'

'Do the Mori brothers still eat here?'

There was a brief silence.

'Now and then. Personally, I've never liked them much, especially not Manuel. That kid always wants to impress everybody. He drives flashy cars and, from the look of him, you'd think he was as rich as Croesus. But it's Jo, his brother, who runs the wholesale business. Manuel barely sets foot in Rue du Caire. Most of the time he's swanning around Deauville, Le Touquet, places like that.'

'With women?'

'He can't have any trouble on that front because he's good-looking, but I don't know that he has anything serious on the go. Not that it's any of my business, though. The boss seemed to have a bit of a soft spot for him.'

'One thing surprises me. Monsieur Maurice seemed very in love and very jealous of his wife. He left her alone at home with the cook and the maid. But if I understood the cashier correctly yesterday, he never bothered to call her, even just to say goodnight.'

'How would you know?'

'What do you mean? Was the cashier lying?'

'She wasn't lying but she doesn't know any more about it than I do. The boss would often ask to have an open line put through to his phone and then go to his office. So he could have called whoever he wanted.'

'Was that a regular occurrence?'

'Once or twice an evening.'

'Do you think he was calling his wife?'

'He may have been taking care of other things, but he must have called her too.'

'And if she hadn't been there?'

The head waiter looked at him without answering.

'You have to assume that never happened,' he muttered after a while.

It wasn't hard to guess what he was thinking.

The cashier had taken up her post behind the little counter reserved for her and was getting the till ready.

'Do you mind if I go and have a quick chat with her?'

'Make yourself at home, detective chief inspector.'

When Maigret tried to pay for the two beers, he added:

'On the house.'

'Good evening, mademoiselle.'

'Good evening, inspector.'

'You told me yesterday, or rather this morning, that Monsieur Maurice wasn't in the habit of asking you to make calls for him.'

'That's correct.'

'And yet he called his wife almost every evening . . .'

'I wouldn't know about that. He sometimes asked me to put his phone through to an outside line. In that case I had no way of knowing who he called.'

'Was it always at the same time?'

'Never before eleven. Generally around twelve thirty.'

'Did he ring out of town?'

'Sometimes. I know from the phone bills because it was my job to pay them.'

'Did he always call the same place?'

'No. The one that came up most was a little village which I could barely find on the map: Les Eglandes, in the Oise.'

'Do you know that your next boss is going to be a woman rather than a man?'

'I thought as much.'

'How do you feel about that?'

'It's never pleasant . . . Well, we'll see.'

There were two customers at the bar now. Maigret and Janvier got into the car.

'To the office, chief?'

'I'm debating whether to go home . . . I'm starting to feel sluggish . . . And it's exhausting asking questions without knowing where they're leading.'

'Do you think Marcia's murder was premeditated?'

'No. Or else it's one of the most extraordinary crimes I've come across.'

'You keep talking about the Mori brothers.'

'Because I've had my eye on them for a long time. There's a reason I talked about furniture just now, to Madame Marcia's great surprise.

'Maurice was a rough diamond, with no schooling in the arts. And yet almost overnight he filled his apartment with genuine antiques which could almost be museum pieces.'

'The chateau gang?'

'Why not? It's impeccable taste, at least as far as I can tell. I'm going to have the apartment gone over by an expert. If the furniture and art were bought from dealers, there'll be receipts somewhere.'

'Do you think Line Marcia knows?'

'I wouldn't swear she does, but then again I wouldn't swear she doesn't either. She made a great point of telling us that she never went to buy them with her husband.'

It was rush hour, and it took them almost three-quarters of an hour to get to Boulevard Richard-Lenoir.

'See you tomorrow, Janvier.'

'See you tomorrow, chief.'

Maigret mopped his face before setting off up the stairs. He was dripping with sweat.

'Someone called three times but refused to leave a number for you to call them back. He'll try to get hold of you later.'

'Man's voice? Woman's?'

'It could have been either. He or she kept saying that it was extremely urgent, a matter of life or death.'

Just when Maigret was finally about to sit down for dinner by the open window, when he was finally relaxing . . .

3.

It wasn't until around nine that the ringing telephone echoed through the apartment. Maigret hurried over to pick it up, switching off the television on the way.

'Hello? Detective Chief Inspector Maigret?'

The famous voice, at last.

'You don't know me but I know you. I saw you again this afternoon when you visited Line Marcia, and then when you went to La Sardine.'

People had described an indeterminate voice, one that could have been a man's or a woman's. To Maigret, though, it sounded more like a boy's voice that was breaking, and a meaningless phrase came into his head: a nutcracker voice. It constantly veered from bass to treble and back again.

'Who are you?'

'My name wouldn't mean anything to you. Inspector Louis doesn't know it either, even though I've been calling him on and off for years now. I tried to reach him today, but he's not at home or in his office. So I decided to speak to you directly. So come on, tell me, when are you arresting him?'

'Who?'

'You know as well as I do. Manuel Mori, because it's the older brother this is all about.'

Maigret heard the clatter of coins. The stranger was calling from a telephone box.

'It's very urgent, detective chief inspector. It's a matter of life or death for me. You've put detectives on the tail of the two brothers. I spotted them immediately. The Moris are professionals and they're bound to have spotted them too. They'll realize someone's talked, and those guys know me. They'll be sure to think of me.

'Please, at least arrest Manuel. He's the most dangerous. He's the one who shot Monsieur Maurice.'

'Why?'

There was a sudden silence at the other end of the line, and Maigret frowned. He waited for a long time but the telephone remained mute.

There was no sound of coins this time, just a void, an agonizing void.

'Did he tell you who he was?' Madame Maigret asked.

'No. He knows a lot and he's in danger.'

In the end he went to bed feeling disgruntled and worried. He couldn't protect someone if he didn't know his name or what he looked like.

When he went into Quai des Orfèvres the following morning, it was already hot. He spotted Inspector Louis waiting for him on one of the benches in the long corridor.

'Are you here to see me?'

'Yes, sir.'

'Have you heard from your public-spirited informer?'

'Yes. He rang me early in the evening. He broke off his conversation with you because he saw someone he knew through the window of the telephone box and he didn't want them to see him. He also told me that he wasn't going to be in touch again until the Mori brothers are arrested. He's going into hiding.'

'Do you really think he's in danger?'

'Yes. Otherwise he wouldn't talk about it.'

'What are the rumours going around Montmartre?'

'That only one of them, Manuel or Monsieur Maurice, was going to come out of it alive. They were both armed. I suppose Mori was the quickest.'

'What about the motive?'

'Whenever I bring it up, people just smile.'

'Do you think Mori was Line Marcia's lover?'

'It occurred to me. If he was, I suspect she was risking her life as well as her fortune.'

'Have you been to Rue Ballu this morning?'

'The door was already draped in black, and people are filing in and out.'

'Did you recognize anyone?'

'It was a mixture: tradesmen, restaurant owners, night-club hostesses, pimps.'

'I'd like to see for myself.'

He called Janvier and asked him to get a car ready in the courtyard.

'Come with me, Monsieur Louis. You know these people better than I do.'

Little groups were standing around on the pavement in Rue Ballu as if it was the day of the funeral. Monsieur Maurice's dramatic death was big news all over Montmartre, and people were discussing it in hushed tones.

'Let's go in.'

They went up to the second floor. Silence reigned in the

stairwell. The apartment door was half-open. From the hall they could smell candles and chrysanthemums. There were more flowers and wreaths than places to put them, and there was no question now of the vast drawing room needing greenery to make it look less bare.

Line was standing in full mourning by the door, bowing her head to each visitor and shaking their outstretched hands. Her face was frozen, inscrutable.

When she recognized Maigret, she sneered contemptuously, as if to reproach him for coming and having no respect for death.

'My sincere condolences,' he mumbled.

'They're no use to me.'

The coffin was still open, and Maurice Marcia could be seen dressed in a suit, his face peaceful, with what seemed like a sarcastic smile on his lips. The drawing room was hung with a black fabric decorated with silver teardrops and lit by a dozen candles, whose scent spread through the whole building.

The visitors stood in contemplation for a moment, looking at the dead man dressed as if for a grand ceremony.

'Do you recognize anyone?' whispered Maigret.

'A couple of pimps. The owner of the Sans-Gêne, with his wife who runs the place with him.'

'Do you think this will go on all day?'

'Definitely. And the church of Notre-Dame-de-Lorette won't be big enough tomorrow.'

They lingered among the people on the other side of the street, watching the visitors go in and out.

'Here they are.'

A red Jaguar had just stopped at the corner of the street, and two men, still very young, got out. They were both elegant and handsome, and there was something defiant about their expressions.

They were well known and they knew it. They walked down the middle of the street, discreetly acknowledging people to left and right. When the older brother saw Maigret, he hesitated for a second then walked over.

'You're going to a lot of trouble having me and my brother followed, detective chief inspector. I could spare you the expense of these tails by telling you what's in my diary. This afternoon, for instance, I'll be at Rue du Caire with Jo because we've got a big delivery. Tomorrow, after the funeral, I'll be going to Bandol . . .

'As for you, Louis, you just go on ferreting around all over the place and listening to the gossip, why don't you. Marcia deserved better than that.'

Apparently very pleased with himself, he turned back to his brother and went into the building.

'You can see the kind of man he is,' muttered Inspector Louis. 'A young wolf with sharp fangs who thinks he's smarter than anyone else.'

'I'd like to question his concierge.'

'She only works during the day. Nights, it's her husband who sleeps on a camp bed in the lodge. He's called Victor, and everyone in the neighbourhood knows him. He's a chronic drinker who spends his days going from bar to bar.'

'Can we get hold of him?'

'We can try. Square La Bruyère and Place Saint-Georges are the places to start.'

In each of the bars Inspector Louis drank a strawberry Vichy, while Maigret made do with a total of two glasses of beer.

'You haven't seen Victor, have you?'

'He came by half an hour ago. He must have been starting his rounds because he wasn't drunk yet.'

When the two men caught up with him in the sixth bar, he was well on his way.

'Oh look! Inspector Louis. A quarter bottle of Vichy for the inspector! What about you, big man?'

He was the sort of wreck to be found under the bridges. His shirt was open, showing his chest, and one of the pockets had come unstitched and was hanging off.

'I bet you've come to see me. Who's this guy? A doctor?'

'Why would a doctor be interested in you?'

'It wouldn't be the first time. They try to lock me up even though I'm the gentlest soul in the world.'

That made him laugh.

'This is Detective Chief Inspector Maigret.'

'I've heard that name. What does Detective Chief Inspector Maigret want from me?'

'You sleep in the lodge at night, don't you?'

'Since my wife got sick, and the doctors told her to rest.'

'How many tenants are there in the building?'

'I've never counted. Two apartments on each floor and roughly three people in each apartment. Do the sums yourself. Maths and me fell out a long time ago.'

'Do you know Monsieur Mori well?'

'I'd say he was a friend.'

'Why?'

'Because from time to time when he comes in he slips me a bottle. It never occurs to anyone else that I might be thirsty.'

'Does he usually come in late?'

'Depends what you call late. Give me another, Gaston.'

The cheap red trickled down his unshaven chin.

'Midnight?'

'Midnight what?'

'Does he come in around midnight?'

'Or five in the morning. Depends on the night. When his girl comes to see him . . .'

'You mean he comes in with women?'

'No, monsieur. Not with women. With a woman.'

'Always the same one, then.'

'Always the same one, then. Exactly.'

'Tall?'

'Not quite as tall as him but taller than me.'

'Thin? Blonde?'

'What's wrong with thin and blonde?'

'Does she spend the whole night with him?'

'Come on! You're way off. She never stays more than an hour or two.'

'Do you know her name?'

'I'm not the police, am I? What about you, do you know my name?'

'Victor . . .'

'Victor who? You think I don't have a surname like

everybody else? Well, I'm called Macoulet, same as my father and mother, and I was born near Arras. What do you say to that?'

'Did he slip you a bottle when he came in with her?'

'Hey, I hadn't thought of that! Could be. The last time it was.'

'When was that?'

'Yesterday? No, the day before yesterday. I'm losing my sense of time a bit, the days and nights are all the same. It was when the people on the first floor had a soirée, as they called it. The ceiling shook over my head, and champagne corks were going off all night.'

'What floor does Monsieur Mori live on?'

'The third . . . Beautiful apartment, I can tell you. He didn't buy that furniture on the cheap or from department stores. The bedroom is completely hung with yellow silk, for one thing . . . What do you say to that?'

'Does he come in at the same time as her?'

'He always comes in at the same time as her. Maybe he's afraid someone will steal her.'

'Did anyone else come in that night when Mori and his lady friend were upstairs?'

'Let me think . . . It's crazy how thirsty thinking makes you. If you could treat me to a bottle of . . .'

Maigret signalled to the owner in a blue apron to serve him.

'You know, I never see the people who go past. When they ring the bell I'm not always completely awake . . . You mustn't tell the property manager that, he's a bastard . . . Anyway, they come in and say a name as they go by the glass door. That night the man, because he was on his own, said: "Mori."

'I thought: "That's odd. Mori came in a minute ago with his girl."

'But he might have gone out again to buy a bottle . . . Or else it wasn't him who came in, it was his brother. Because there's two of them . . . You know there's two of them, don't you? Anyway, the guy pushed the light button and went up . . .'

'By the stairs or the lift?'

'I wouldn't know about that. I went back to sleep.'

'Did you see him leave?'

'The door opens from the inside when you go out.'

'Did anyone make a noise as they left?'

'God, yes! The gang having a wild time on the first floor. They were all completely drunk, even the women, shrieking their way down the stairs.'

'Did you get up to have a look at them?'

'No. I heard the door shut and didn't give it another thought.'

'What about the girlfriend?'

'What girlfriend? You've got one bad habit, inspector. You talk about everyone at the same time. Are you talking about the people on the first floor or Mori?'

'Manuel Mori and his mistress.'

'Right. That's clearer for a start, although you've forgotten the brother . . .'

'Did he leave on his own?'

'The brother? I don't even know if it was the brother . . .'

'Another glass of beer,' ordered Maigret, his forehead covered with sweat. 'Fine. Let's say the visitor.'

'I didn't hear him go past the lodge when he left.'

'What about the girl . . .'

'If you knew her, you wouldn't be talking about a girl. She's a real lady . . .'

'The lady, then.'

'She wasn't up there more than half an hour.'

'Did you see her leave?'

'No. Definitely not. If I had to get up to take a look at everyone who goes out, I might as well not have a bed.'

'Did Mori come down with a heavy bundle after that?'

'Sorry, didn't see. Mori or the bundle. But I heard the car starting up.'

'Mori's car?'

'Yes. A little red car, very powerful, that makes a lot of noise when it starts up.'

'What time did he come back after that?'

'I don't know. But when he said his name on the way past I started to think that lot upstairs were pushing it a bit. If it wasn't for the drink . . .'

'Was there a second bottle?'

'No. But the first one wasn't a cheap red like this. It was cognac.'

'Thank you, Victor,' Maigret called after paying for the drinks.

Once out in the street, he muttered:

'It seems that your informer . . .'

'What do you mean, my informer?'

'The character who rings you up with tips every now and then.'

'I've never asked him to. I don't know him.'

'Pity, because he seems to know a lot. After what I've just heard, I'm beginning to understand why he's afraid. Do you think the Moris could kill him?'

'Or have him killed. I think they're capable of anything.'

'I'm debating whether to ask the examining magistrate for an arrest warrant.'

'For both of them?'

'If the younger one is as dangerous as Manuel.'

'What shall I do?'

'Go on asking around the neighbourhood. It's buzzing, that will help. People will be talking among themselves, trading bits of information.'

'Are you going to arrest them today?'

'I'll go and see them at Rue du Caire first.'

Maigret nevertheless looked in on the examining magistrate on the way. Bouteille, as he was called, was in his fifties and had known Maigret for a long time.

'Have you got the murderer for me already?'

'Not exactly. But I'm starting to get a clearer picture of it all.'

Maigret said what he knew. The two men sat across the desk from one another, smoking their pipes.

When Maigret had finished, the magistrate growled:

'It's not much in the way of proof.'

'I'd like to have an arrest warrant in my pocket when I go to see them. And a search warrant.'

'For both brothers?'

'That would be better. I don't know where the inform-
er's hideout is. Jo is apparently as dangerous as Manuel.'
Bouteille turned to his clerk.
'Make out two arrest warrants in the names of the Mori
brothers, Manuel and Joseph.'
Maigret provided their addresses.
The magistrate led him to the door.
'The case is going to cause a stir.'
'It already has.'
'I know, I've read the papers.'
One of them had the chilly headline:

Maurice Marcia: gang boss killed by rival?

Another referred to all Pigalle's little mysteries and the
part played by the police, their tendency to turn a blind
eye.

The investigation promises to be difficult, and it is legiti-
mate to ask whether we will ever get to the bottom of
this affair.

Tomorrow's funeral is likely to attract a considerable
crowd since La Sardine's owner had friends not only in
the neighbourhood but all over Paris. Not that they'll all
be attending, it's true.

As for Detective Chief Inspector Maigret, he refuses
to make any sort of statement. So far, it's not even known
if he will be going to Bandol tomorrow.

When questioned, his only answer is: 'The investigation is proceeding.'

The Moris' warehouse was on the edge of Les Halles, which was physically intact – they hadn't started demolishing the buildings – but silent now that trading had moved to Rungis.

Rue du Caire was one of the many streets where you found wholesalers and warehouses rubbing shoulders with short-stay hotels and seedy bars.

In a year it would probably all be a heap of rubble.

When Maigret got out of the taxi, he spotted a couple of detectives kicking their heels on the pavement. He wondered for a moment why there were two of them, then realized that one was watching Manuel Mori and the other his brother Jo.

'You know you've been rumbled, boys?'

'That's why we're not hiding. The older brother strolled up to me, calm as you like, blew his cigarette smoke in my face like in a movie and said:

' "No point playing hide-and-seek, flatfoot. I know you're here. I'm not going to try and give you the slip." '

The warehouse was a long bare room without a shopfront, which must have had a metal shutter which was locked at night. In the middle Maigret could see a lorry unloading. A man in grey overalls on the lorry was throwing crates of fruit down to his partner, who was catching them and stacking them against a wall.

A few metres away, his hands in his pockets, a cigarette between his lips, Jo Mori was watching the unloading with a distracted look on his face. He didn't frown when he saw Maigret or make any move towards him.

In the right-hand corner of the warehouse, near the

street, there was a glassed-in office, in which Manuel was going through a pile of receipts, his hat pushed back on his head. He had obviously seen Maigret too but was unconcerned.

Maigret pushed open the office door, took the only free chair and sat down, then began filling his pipe.

Manuel gave in first, muttering:

'I was expecting you.'

Maigret still didn't say anything.

'In fact, I've just called my lawyer. He's another one who thinks you talk too much, you and that inspector in mourning who's been skulking around Montmartre for ever. You both ask too many people too many questions.'

Apparently taking no notice, Maigret carefully lit his pipe.

'Sometimes sneaky questions can do as much damage as accusations, and then that becomes slander.

'As long as my brother and me are the only ones involved, we couldn't care less, but now you're implicating other people. As for the Flea, he's meddled in other people's business so he could be in big trouble.'

And with that Maigret finally found out from one of the Mori brothers, without asking, the identity of the man who had rung him the previous day and who rang Inspector Louis with tips on a more or less regular basis.

'Where were you the day before yesterday at half past midnight?'

'At home.'

'No. That's where you were half an hour earlier, and you weren't on your own.'

'I can have whatever guests I want.'

65

'But not murder anyone who comes to your apartment.'

'I haven't murdered a soul.'

'And I'm sure you don't have a firearm of any kind, even a .32 revolver.'

'What would I do with that?'

'You found a use for it that night. Although you could always plead self-defence, it's true.'

'I don't need to defend myself against anyone.'

'I'd like to see your apartment.'

'Go and ask a magistrate for a warrant, then.'

Maigret took the warrant out of his pocket and handed it to Manuel, along with the two arrest warrants.

Mori clearly wasn't expecting this. He started noticeably, spilling cigarette ash on his suit jacket.

'What does this mean?'

'What these forms generally mean.'

'Are you arresting me?'

'I don't know yet. Probably. Are you still saying I can't see your apartment?'

Manuel stood up, trying to regain his swagger. He half opened the door.

'Hey, Jo! Come here a minute.'

His brother had taken off his jacket and rolled up the sleeves of his white shirt.

'You recognize the colour of these forms, don't you? There's one for you, one for me, and another for both of us, the search warrant. You haven't got a body hidden in your wardrobe, have you?'

The younger Mori didn't join in the joke but read the warrants carefully.

'Now what?' he asked.

It wasn't clear whether he was talking to his brother or Maigret.

'After I've finished with your brother I'll come to your hotel. Go and wait for me there.'

'Do you have a car?' asked Manuel.

'A taxi.'

'Wouldn't you rather I drove you?'

'No. I do want you to follow me, though. Don't try to overtake the taxi.'

Maigret picked up the inspector tailing Manuel on the way.

'Where are we going?'

'To his place, Square La Bruyère.'

'He's following us.'

'I asked him to.'

It was a stone's throw from Rue Fontaine. The Marcias' apartment on Rue Ballu was similarly close to the restaurant. And Jo lived at the Hôtel des Iles, Avenue Trudaine, only five minutes away.

'The funeral's tomorrow, isn't it?'

'The service is tomorrow, but then they're taking him to Bandol, where he'll be buried.'

The six-floor building was modern, luxurious.

'What shall I do? Shall I go up with you?'

'I'd rather you stayed down here.'

The red Jaguar stopped behind the taxi.

'I'll show you the way,' Manuel said.

As they passed the lodge, the curtain twitched.

'It's on the fourth floor.'

'I know.'

'Doesn't it bother you, taking the lift with me?'

'Not at all.'

'You might be afraid. I'm younger and stronger than you.'

Maigret just gave him the sort of look you'd give a bragging child.

Manuel took a key from his pocket, opened the door, then stepped aside to let Maigret go in first.

'As you can see, I don't have a maid. A nice lady comes and does the cleaning every day, but as I'm often asleep at this time of day, she only comes in the afternoon.'

The drawing room wasn't large, especially compared to the one in Rue Ballu, but it was furnished with equal refinement. It led into a dining room with a still life by Chardin of pheasants in a basket, which Maigret thought looked genuine.

'Chardin?'

'I believe so.'

'Do you like oil paintings?'

'I like them well enough. Just because we sell tomatoes and fruit doesn't mean we can't appreciate the arts.'

His tone was bantering. In the bedroom the bed was unmade. It was the only modern room in the apartment, very light and cheerful. It gave on to a bathroom which was large enough to have a punchbag set up in the middle.

'Tour over. You've seen everything.'

'Not quite. Something's missing from the bedroom.'

'What?'

'There used to be a small rug in the middle of the room, where that lighter patch is on the carpet.'

Maigret bent down.

'Besides there are still coloured threads in the pile here which are probably from the missing rug.'

'Look around for it, then.'

'I'm not going to make a fool of myself like that. Do you mind?'

He picked up the telephone and asked for the Police Judiciaire, then the laboratory.

'Is that you, Moers? Maigret here. I'd like you to come with two or three men to Square La Bruyère. You'll find one of our inspectors at the door. Go up to the fourth floor. What am I looking for? Whatever you can find . . .'

Manuel wasn't so arrogant now.

'They'll turn the whole apartment upside down.'

'Probably.'

'I can tell you straight off, this rug you're going on about never existed.'

'Then we'll find out where those coloured threads are from.'

'I've got a friend whose coat—'

'No. Madame Marcia – Line, if you'd rather – is a woman of taste who'd never wear a brightly coloured coat mixing greens, reds and yellows like that.'

'I suppose my lawyer is allowed to be present during the search, is he?'

'I don't see any objection personally.'

It was Manuel's turn to make a telephone call.

'Hello, could I have a word with Maître Garcin, please . . . Manuel Mori . . . It's very urgent.'

He was becoming agitated.

'Garcin? Listen, my friend, I'm calling from home. The detective chief inspector has a search warrant. He's found some threads in the carpet he isn't happy with, and now he's called the people from Criminal Records. You wouldn't mind coming over here, would you?

'What's that? I have to let them search the furniture and the drawers? That's not all, though. He's got arrest warrants in my brother's name and in mine.

'No. He said he doesn't know if he'll use them yet . . . Listen, if I haven't called you before, let's say, four this afternoon, do whatever you have to do to get us out. I don't want to spend the night in the Mousetrap. Besides, the funeral's tomorrow, and I was planning to go on to Bandol for the burial . . . She's well, yes. Thanks, my friend. See you soon.'

His conversation with his lawyer had bucked him up a bit.

He was surprised when Maigret said:

'If you'd told me you were going to Bandol . . .'

'What difference would that have made?'

'I wouldn't have bothered with the warrants just now. I wasn't thinking of Line, who I'm sure will need you.'

'What are you implying?'

'What everybody in Pigalle knows. The days of you having two or three girlfriends a week are over.'

'My private life is my business.'

'It's one thing to sleep with a friend's wife, that's true, but to shoot him in the chest . . .'

The doorbell rang. Moers was accompanied by two men carrying small cases.

'This way. It's in the bedroom. No point asking what used to be there, where that light patch is.'

'A rug, naturally.'

'There are still some threads in the pile. I'd like you to collect and examine them. Generally speaking, the whole apartment needs a good going over. I'd be interested if you found any plans of houses or chateaus, say, or correspondence with foreign antique dealers or art dealers.'

This time Mori was stunned and made no attempt to hide it.

'This is news to me. What's it all about?'

'It's nothing yet, just a vague thought, but it could turn into something. I'll leave you to get on with it, Moers. I've got something else to take care of. I may need you for that as well.'

Turning to Manuel, he said:

'I'll leave you too. Until you hear otherwise, you're a free man but you're not allowed to leave town.'

'What about going to Bandol?'

'I'll tell you tomorrow morning.'

'Can I call Line?'

'You were just there . . .'

Manuel shrugged.

'Given what you know, there's no point denying it. Especially because we haven't done anything wrong.'

'I hope not.'

A few minutes later, Maigret was walking into the Hôtel des Iles. It wasn't a luxury establishment but it was comfortable and very clean and its clientele was no doubt all permanent residents. He went to the office.

'Jo Mori, please.'

The young girl on the other side of the counter smiled at him.

'Third floor. Number 22, Monsieur Maigret.'

'Did he tell you he was expecting me?'

'No. He told me he was expecting someone. But I recognized you the moment you came through the door.'

Maigret took the lift, knocked at 22, and the door opened immediately. It was Jo, who had left Rue du Caire to be home when he arrived.

'What have you done with my brother?'

'I've left him at his apartment. Admittedly with some specialists from Criminal Records who are going to search it thoroughly.'

'Didn't you arrest him?'

'Line will need him tomorrow. He has to go to Bandol. What about you?'

'I wasn't planning to. Which Line are you talking about?'

'Forget it. It's already old news. Your brother has admitted they're lovers.'

'I don't believe you.'

They were in a small dove-grey sitting room which was rather old-fashioned but no less pleasant for it. Jo hesitated, then reached for the telephone and dialled his brother's number.

Clasping his hands behind his back, Maigret looked around. He opened a door at random and found himself face to face with a young woman who was wearing only a loosely tied nightgown.

'You're Jo's mistress, I suppose? That's a stupid question because here you are in his bedroom, not far from the unmade bed, with some of your clothes on an armchair.'

'Is there any harm in that?'

'None at all. How old are you?'

'Twenty-two.'

He heard Jo's voice behind him.

'He's already with her . . . I didn't have time . . . What's this about you, though? Is it true that he's letting you go to Bandol and that you told him about Line? . . . You should have warned me . . . I don't know . . . He's chatting with her in the bedroom . . . You know her, she could talk for hours on end. Trouble is, I haven't found a deaf-mute I like yet.'

He quickly hung up, and his silhouette appeared in the bedroom door.

The young girl was saying:

'I'm called Marcelle . . . Marcelle Vainer. I'm from Béziers but I came up to Paris the first chance I got.'

'How long have you been with Jo?'

'A month, and I'm not getting my hopes up. I reckon I've got another month.'

'Cover yourself up,' the young man said drily.

Turning to Maigret, he complained:

'If you told me what you're looking for exactly, we could save some time. You know I've got a truck unloading, and the merchandise will have to be delivered after that.'

73

Maigret continued talking to Marcelle as if he hadn't heard.

'Where were you the night before last?'

'From when?'

'From eleven in the evening.'

'We went to the cinema, Jo and me. We came back straight afterwards because he was tired.'

'What time did he get a telephone call?'

She opened her mouth, then shut it, looking questioningly at Mori.

'No harm in that,' Mori said. 'It was my brother calling to say he was going on a trip to the countryside in the next couple of days.'

'To Bandol?' Maigret asked sardonically.

'Bandol or somewhere. He didn't tell me.'

'If he'd said Bandol that would have been a premonition, because Maurice Marcia wasn't dead at that point.'

'How would I know?'

'The story was all over the papers yesterday, and they gave the time of death. Around twelve thirty.'

'Maybe. It doesn't interest me.'

'Don't you have any oil paintings here?'

'What oil paintings?'

'I don't know. There are a lot of art lovers in this business.'

'Not me.'

'And your furniture is good solid hotel furniture.'

'What else would it be?'

'Is this where you keep the receipts and the business papers?'

'They're all in Rue du Caire, in the office, of course.'

'Do you work, Mademoiselle Marcelle?'

'Not at the moment.'

'What did you do before you met this young man?'

'I was a barmaid at a bar on Rue de Ponthieu. Maybe I made a mistake giving up my job.'

'I agree.'

'What do you think I should do?'

'Go on then!' Jo interrupted, his fists clenched.

'Steady, son. I'm not taking you in today. Get on with your life. But don't take it into your head to leave Paris.

'Oh, and one more piece of advice: don't touch a hair on the Flea's head if you see him. That could prove very costly.'

Maigret went downstairs, filling his pipe. He had forgotten the young girl at reception and was surprised when a cheery youthful voice called out, 'Goodbye, Monsieur Maigret.'

4.

As soon as he got to Quai des Orfèvres, Maigret called Janvier into his office.

'Any news on the Marcia case?'

'Just a call from Inspector Louis, who'd like to talk to you.'

'Is he in his office?'

'No. He'll be in the Restaurant du Rhône on Boulevard de Clichy at twelve thirty.'

'Would you like to have lunch with me?'

'Happy to. My wife is at her mother's today, so I would have eaten out anyway.'

Maigret called his wife.

'I've got a lot of work so I won't be coming home for lunch.'

She had known as much. Whenever an investigation reached a certain point he felt the need to play truant, as it were, and have lunch with one of his colleagues at the Brasserie Dauphine.

It was his way of staying in the swing of things. The two men slowly strolled to the brasserie and stopped at the bar, where several men from Quai des Orfèvres were already having a drink.

'For a change, I'll have a small pastis,' muttered Maigret.

A rare event these days. Since his old friend Pardon had warned him about his health he drank much less than before and sometimes kept a pipe clamped between his teeth long after it had gone out.

'You don't know what Louis wants, do you?'

'Well, you know him, always very mysterious.'

'He's a brilliant man but he could never join the team. He needs to work alone.'

The owner came up and shook hands. He had lost his hair so gradually that no one noticed he was completely bald these days.

'What's for lunch?'

'*Andouillette*. But if you'd rather a steak . . .'

'I'll have the *andouillette*,' Maigret decided.

'I will too,' Janvier echoed.

They went into the restaurant, where only four tables were occupied, two by lawyers. It was a home from home for everyone in their world. Maigret had his corner by the window, from where he could watch the Seine and passing boats. He watched the boats go by from his office too. He had done so for over thirty years, but he never grew tired of it.

'Would you call Orly when you get back to the office, please? I'd like a seat on a plane to Marseille tomorrow. Preferably around midday.'

'Are you going to Bandol?'

'Yes. Unofficially, of course, as it's outside our jurisdiction.'

'I know there's an Air Inter flight . . .'

'It's twelve thirty now. Will you give Inspector Louis a

call too and ask him to come to my office after he's had lunch?'

By one fifteen the Widower was facing Maigret across his desk. The window was open and they could hear the leaves on the trees rustling outside. Maigret had taken off his jacket. Louis was dressed in black as usual, including his tie.

'I got a call this morning from my anonymous caller's girlfriend.'

Maigret couldn't help smiling.

'She didn't tell me her name. She's worried because she hasn't heard from her boyfriend for forty-eight hours.'

Maigret calmly waited for him to finish.

'There's another, vaguer rumour doing the rounds. At least three or four crooks have suddenly felt the need to leave Montmartre and they all just happen to be friends of the Mori brothers.'

'I have some news for you too, inspector. I know who your anonymous caller is.'

Louis turned bright red. It seemed inconceivable to him that Maigret could have made an identification in twenty-four hours when he had failed for years.

'Who is it?'

'Do you know the Flea?'

'Everyone in Montmartre knows him.'

'It's him. I heard it from Manuel Mori himself, who either let it slip or thought I knew already.'

Maigret had known the man, who was nicknamed the Flea because he was barely one metre fifty tall, for almost thirty years. He was thin as well as short, with a strange face that was almost entirely taken up by his mouth. It looked as if it was made of India rubber and could take on any imaginable expression in an instant.

He had started out as a messenger boy at the Rat de Cave, a club on Place Pigalle that was very elegant at the time, with a clientele who mainly wore evening dress. He stood at the door, dressed in the club's red uniform, with a short jacket and braided cap, ready to take customers' messages all over town.

After a while, the Rat de Cave had gone under. The Flea, whose real name was Justin Crotton, had then spent the next couple of years working in a brasserie on Rue Victor-Massé, where all the local crime bosses went.

He was still as thin and agile as ever, still able to slip in anywhere, but his face had become lined. From a distance he looked like a boy. Close up he showed every one of his forty-five or forty-six years.

'To think I didn't recognize his voice,' moaned Louis.

'He must do his best to disguise it.'

'Not really. Now you've told me, it all comes back to me. I can't forgive myself for not thinking of him.'

'How has he been earning a living recently?'

'He was hanging around with a hostess from the Canary in Rue Pigalle, who lives in Rue Fromentin.'

'Her pimp?'

'Pretty much. I don't know exactly. It's quite strange for a good-looking girl like her to set up house with that little runt. He was born in Paris, on Boulevard de la Chapelle, and I hardly need tell you his mother's profession. She sent him to one of her sisters in Saint-Mesmin-le-Vieux in the

Vendée. When he was fourteen he came back to Paris and fended for himself.'

'He's in danger,' Maigret said gravely.

'You think the Moris would dare . . .'

'They'd keep out of it. They've got enough killers at their disposal to deal with an awkward witness.'

Inspector Louis still couldn't get over it.

'The Flea! No one suspects him for a minute. He's considered a harmless creature, not even a man exactly, more a kind of boy with a wrinkled face. He hangs around all the crooks who don't think twice about talking in front of him.

'I think he dreams of being accepted as one of them. I wouldn't be surprised if they didn't use him as a lookout from time to time.'

'What's his girlfriend called?'

'Blanche Pigoud. Number 28, Rue Fromentin. It's seconds from Boulevard de Clichy, where I had lunch.'

'Do you know her?'

'Only by sight, as I've never had anything on her.'

'She must go to bed late. We'll probably find her at home now.'

'Unless it's her day to get her hair done. Those girls only get up early to go to the hairdresser.'

Maigret called Janvier.

'Will you come with us? We're off to Montmartre again.'

'Shall I get a car?'

'Of course.'

All three of them set off. It was a glorious day, a little too hot for May, and the forecast was storms.

Rue Fromentin was quiet. Number 28 was a relatively new and reassuringly sturdy apartment block.

'Shall we all go up?'

'I'll go up first on my own so as not to scare her. No, actually, it would be better if Inspector Louis came with me, because she rang him.'

'Second floor on the street side,' the concierge told them.

There was a smell of cooking on the stairs, and a baby could be heard crying somewhere. Maigret rang the bell. It took an age before rather a plump young woman, who was only wearing a light dressing gown, opened the door a chink.

She recognized Inspector Louis.

'Have you found him?'

'Not yet, but Detective Chief Inspector Maigret would like to talk to you.'

'Look at the state I'm in. I was asleep. I haven't even combed my hair.'

'We'll give you a moment,' Maigret replied amiably.

The girl had an open, even slightly naive face. She must have been about twenty-five, and the life she was leading hadn't robbed her of her freshness yet.

'Come in, make yourself comfortable. I'll be there in a second.'

She went into a bedroom which must have led through to the bathroom.

If Maigret hadn't been used to the kind of women respectable ladies regarded with contempt, he would have been surprised by the décor surrounding them.

The living room was comfortably furnished, with the sort of so-called modern furniture you would have found in half the apartments in Paris. All of it was carefully polished, the floor too. There was also a slight smell of disinfectant.

Pushing open a door, Maigret found an immaculate kitchen without a hint of mess to be seen.

'Would you like a cup of coffee?' asked the young woman when she reappeared. She was still wearing nothing under her dressing gown, but she had splashed some cold water over her face and put on a little make-up.

'No, thank you.'

'Do you mind if I make myself one? In my job you can't always refuse a drink. Bob gives me cold tea instead of whisky whenever he can, but with some customers you just can't get out of it. If you want, there's some beer in the refrigerator. Justin loves beer and is always hoping it will help him put on weight. Do you know that he weighs less than forty-two kilos?

'He nearly became a jockey, but his apprenticeship only lasted a couple of days because he was afraid of horses.

'He's not afraid of Pigalle's hard men, though.'

She had switched on an electric coffee-maker. The kitchen was equipped with all the latest appliances.

'You didn't say about the beer . . .'

'I'd love a glass.'

'Your inspector only drinks Vichy, and I haven't got any here.'

'How do you know he only drinks Vichy?'

'He comes into the Canary every so often. He does the

rounds of all the clubs. He sits in a corner of the bar and listens. He knows much more than you'd think by the look of him.'

'Were you aware of the Flea's telephone calls?'

'Not really.'

She took her coffee into the living room, and Maigret followed with his glass of beer.

'He's a funny boy, as Inspector Louis could tell you, couldn't you, inspector?'

'I've always wondered why you set up home with him . . .'

'For a start because I can't stand most pimps. At heart I'm a nice, respectable girl and I'm never happier than when I'm doing housework.'

They were all sitting in armchairs.

'In my job, though, you need a man.'

'Even if he's a little runt like Justin Crotton?'

'Don't you believe it. In some ways he's still a bit of a child, but he's a lot cannier than he looks.'

She didn't pay any mind to her dressing gown, which hung open. Her skin was very pale, probably very soft.

'His dream was always to become a real gangster. At first, like most of them, he wanted to be a pimp.'

'Which he is now?'

'I let him think so. It helps him take himself seriously. He still does errands left and right, as he did when he was a messenger boy. Occasionally, even with me, he comes over all mysterious and says something cagey like:

' "Don't be surprised if I don't show up for a night or two. We've got something big lined up." '

'Would it be true?'

'It would be true that some gang or other was preparing a job, but he wouldn't be in on it. What I didn't know was that he was ringing the inspector and passing on all the information he'd picked up. That also made him feel important in his own eyes.'

'What happened in the last couple of days? Did he talk about anything?'

'Not really. One morning he came home all overexcited.

' "Something crazy happened last night, something that will be all over the front pages and cause a huge stir."

' "A robbery?"

' "Worse than that. A murder. And the victim is one of the best-known people in the neighbourhood."

' "Can't you tell me his name?"

' "It will be in the papers any moment. It's Monsieur Maurice."

' "From La Sardine?"

' "Yes. And I'm the only person, apart from the murderer and his mistress, who knows who did it."

' "I'd rather not know who that is." '

She took a fresh cigarette, having already lit one when she came out of the bathroom.

'I asked him what he was going to do. He said:

' "Don't worry about me."

' "You're not going to blackmail the guy, at least?"

' "You know that's not my style."

' "Does he know you know?"

' "If he did, I wouldn't be long for this earth . . ." '

She fell silent for a moment, blowing the smoke out in front of her.

'In a way it was the best day of his life.

' "If you knew who it was . . . One of Montmartre's biggest bosses . . . And his mistress . . ."

' "Don't tell me anything."

' "Got it. You'll find out the truth from the papers anyway. If they dare print it . . ."

'He went out that morning and I haven't seen him since. I got strange looks at the Canary that night, and two men I'd never seen before didn't take their eyes off me.

'I stayed at the bar, as I always do. I was joined by a customer from the country who never misses the chance to see me when he's in Paris. We went to the hotel, and when we came out, one of the two men was pacing up and down on the pavement.

'At first I was afraid for the Flea . . . Everyone calls him that, and I've ended up doing so too . . . Anyway, he's quite proud of it. It's a sort of fame. He likes pulling faces too to make people laugh. . . .'

'He called me,' Inspector Louis declared in a neutral voice.

'I thought so. That explains his air of mystery, and what he said when he left. Is he really in danger?'

Maigret answered:

'There's no doubt on that score. Monsieur Maurice's murderer knows it was the Flea who informed on him.'

'What about me? Do you think they'll come after me?'

'Are you still being followed?'

'Last night one of the two men was at the Canary again. He was called to the telephone and then left, but only after giving me a strange look.'

'I may be wrong, but I think they're scattering all over France.'

'What about the Mori brothers?'

'Who told you about them?'

There hadn't been any mention of the brothers in the newspapers or on the radio.

'Everyone's talking about them around here. Have they taken off too?'

'No. But we're keeping an eye on them both.'

'Do you think it's them?'

'I can't answer that question. What time do you normally leave home?'

'I do my shopping locally around two or three, because I like cooking. Then I get dressed up for work around ten in the evening and go to the Canary. I take my seat at the bar and wait. Sometimes I wait for a couple of hours, sometimes only a few minutes, and then sometimes there are nights when I'm there until closing time.'

'There'll be a plainclothes policeman outside your door within an hour. Don't be surprised when he follows you. He'll do everything he can to protect you.'

'Should I go to the funeral tomorrow? Everyone's going.'

'Do that. I'll be there too . . . So will your guardian angel . . .'

'That reminds me of my catechism.'

The two men stood up.

'If you hear anything, ring the Police Judiciaire. Ask to speak to me or one of my men in the Crime Squad. Inspector Louis is hardly ever at his desk.'

'Thank you, detective chief inspector. Goodbye, inspect-or. If you have any news of Justin . . .'

'I hope we won't. He's sensed the danger and gone into hiding. He doesn't need to go far because he knows Mont-martre inside out and there are places where someone like him can stay for weeks without anyone finding him.'

'Let's hope so,' she sighed, touching the wooden table.

They found Janvier outside.

'Well?'

'She's scared, naturally enough, and I don't blame her. Scared for the Flea and for herself. I promised her that in an hour someone from the squad will be at her door and that she'll be followed wherever she goes. Don't forget to see to it when we get to the office. Someone who can get into quite a smart nightclub without attracting attention.'

Maigret turned to Louis.

'In the meantime, you take first watch. As soon as our inspector gets here you'll be free to go.'

'Right, detective chief inspector.'

Once he was behind the steering wheel, Janvier asked:

'What's she like?'

'Lovely. If things had turned out differently for her, probably when she was seventeen or eighteen, she would have been a wonderful wife and homemaker.'

'Did she know?'

'About the Flea's calls? She only suspected something two days ago. It's incredible. That little man with the clown's face has managed to be one of Inspector Louis' informers for years without anyone having a clue. I'm sure he loved the role, and it boosted his self-esteem. Whenever a crook was arrested, he could say to himself: "That's my doing."

'With reason!'

During the afternoon, Maigret went up to the attic of the Palais de Justice, which housed Moers' empire, the Criminal Records laboratory.

Specialists were needed in nine out of ten cases, even if just to lift fingerprints, and yet there couldn't have been as many as a dozen figures in white coats at work in these rooms with sloping ceilings.

'I suppose it's too early to have any news?'

Moers was a skinny, unassuming man whose suit always needed an iron. He had been here for so long that it was hard to imagine Criminal Records without him. He was always ready to work, at any time of day or night. It had to be said that he was also a bachelor, and no one was waiting for him at his student lodgings in the Latin Quarter.

'We've already established something,' he replied in his usual slight monotone. 'Very recently, probably yesterday afternoon in fact, all the furniture was dusted, and the door handles, the ashtrays, every last thing lying around were wiped to get rid of fingerprints.

'The only ones we lifted were the occupant's, Manuel Mori's, whose card I found at Records, and the cleaning lady's, who the concierge told me went to Square La Bruyère yesterday afternoon. I'm ignoring other prints like yours.'

'Didn't they miss any?'

'Not one, chief. It could almost have been a professional job.'

'It was. What is the date of the card you found in Records?'

'It's fourteen years old.'

'Burglary?'

'During the holidays, a town-house on Avenue Hoche.'

'How long did he get?'

'He was only eighteen and had a clean record. He was also thought to be just an accomplice, because five men had done the job.'

'That rings a vague bell, but I didn't deal with it personally.'

'He did a year in prison.'

'Is there any indication that a woman might have been in the apartment, including the bedroom, at all regularly?'

'The cupboards have been gone over with a fine-tooth comb, as it were. No trace of face powder anywhere, no beauty cream, not a single woman's hair.'

'And the carpet?'

'Dorin is probably one of the world's leading authorities on vegetable and animal fibres. It's his pet subject. He spent over an hour studying the carpet with a magnifying glass and collected about thirty barely visible threads. He's been working on them for hours. By threads, I mean silk threads. They're very old, three hundred years at least, and Dorin is convinced they're from a Chinese rug.

'He's still analysing his haul because he wants to be absolutely certain.'

Maigret liked the atmosphere of these attic rooms, where the technicians got on with their work in peace and quiet, far from the public gaze.

Each of them knew what he was supposed to do. Near one of the dormer windows stood the articulated dummy that was constantly used in reconstructions. To find out how a man must have been standing or sitting for him to be stabbed in a certain way, for instance, or for a bullet to have followed a particular trajectory.

'If there are any developments tomorrow, let Janvier know. I'll be in Bandol.'

Moers wasn't the sort to take holidays on the Côte d'Azur. Bandol must have been like a scene from a dream to him.

'It'll be hot,' was all he murmured.

When Maigret told his wife at dinner that he would be going to Bandol the following day, she smiled and said:

'I knew it.'

'How?'

'Because just now the radio said that, although the funeral is at the church of Notre-Dame-de-Lorette tomorrow morning, the actual burial will be in the cemetery in Bandol. What are you hoping to find there?'

'Nothing very specific. Maybe a clue, something small. I'm going for the same reason I'm going to the funeral in the morning.'

'You'll be hot.'

'I may have to spend the night there. It'll depend on flights. I don't feel up to coming back on the train.'

'I'll pack your small blue suitcase.'

'Yes. Just underwear and my wash bag.'

He felt some qualms about going down south at the taxpayers' expense because it wasn't essential. There was every chance he wouldn't learn anything at all in fact.

He slept well, though, as he generally did, and was dazzled by the sun when Madame Maigret brought him his first cup of coffee.

'They're saying it'll be thirty degrees in Marseille today,' she said, smiling.

'What about Paris?'

'Twenty-six. It's the hottest May for thirty-two years.'

'My plane is around midday. I don't know exactly when, Janvier took care of the ticket. I'll just have time to look in at the office before I go to Orly. I'll take my case now.'

'What about lunch? Where and when will you have lunch?'

'If the worst comes to the worst, I'll have a sandwich at the bar at Orly.'

He was heading to the door when she said:

'Aren't you going to kiss me?'

He would have turned back to do so anyway.

'You mustn't worry. I'm not taking a fifty-year-old single-engined aircraft and I'm not setting off round the world.'

He felt a bit emotional all the same, as he did whenever he spent more than a day away from his wife.

Once he was outside in the street he looked up, knowing as he did so that he would see her at the window.

Good thing too, because she was holding up the blue suitcase he had forgotten. They met halfway up the stairs.

It was 9.15 when Janvier came into Maigret's office.

'Apparently the street's already full, and the church won't be able to fit everybody.'

Maigret had been expecting something of the kind, but not quite such a turnout.

'Still no news of the Flea?'

'No. Blanche Pigoud got a call at the Canary last night. She seemed shaken when she went back to the bar, but practically the next moment a customer came and sat beside her.'

'What time did she get home?'

'Around four in the morning.'

'Too bad,' Maigret muttered to himself.

Then he looked for the young woman's number, found it and rang. To his surprise, she didn't take long answering.

'Who is it?' she said in a sleepy voice.

'Detective Chief Inspector Maigret.'

'Have you heard anything?'

'No, you have. Who rang you at the Canary last night?'

'He did, yes . . .'

'Did he tell you where he was?'

'No. He asked if you or Inspector Louis knew about him, and I said yes, you did. Then he asked if you were angry, and I said no to that.'

She sounded like a little girl dazed with sleep.

'You're not angry with him, are you?'

'Is he as scared as he was?'

'Yes. He also wanted to know if there were any strangers hanging around the building.

' "Haven't they arrested anyone yet?"

' "Not as far as I know."

' "Haven't they even searched Manuel Mori's apartment?"

' "I think they have. The detective chief inspector came here with Inspector Louis, but they didn't go into details. Anyway, I've got a policeman watching over me day and night." '

'Did he say anything else?' asked Maigret.

'Only that he was moving to a new place every night. That's all. I couldn't talk much, because a customer had been hovering around for a while.'

'Go back to bed and don't worry about anything. If you have anything new to tell me during the day, call Inspector Janvier at Quai des Orfèvres.'

'Are you going to Bandol?'

It was starting to get on his nerves. Everyone was talking to him about his trip as if he had taken out an advertisement in the papers.

'There you are!' he sighed, looking at Janvier, who was silhouetted against the green of the trees. 'I don't know if it's sensible, but he's changing his hiding place every night.'

'It may not be such a stupid thing to do. There must be a ton of people looking for him.'

If Mori had given the word, as seemed likely, all Montmartre's young thugs would be hunting for the Flea. And, with his physique, he could hardly pass unnoticed in a crowd.

'I'll drop by in a moment to pick up my bag. You'd better give me my plane ticket now.'

Luckily take-off was later than he had feared: 12.55.

'See you soon.'

He took a car to Rue Ballu and told the policeman driving to wait for him by the church.

Over two hundred people were crowded in front of the town-house, although only a few were going in to offer their condolences. There were all sorts, local shopkeepers, pimps, restaurateurs, nightclub owners.

They started bringing down the flowers and needed two cars to carry them and the wreaths.

Then four men brought down the mahogany coffin and slid it into the hearse.

The church was fairly close, not that they could have found cars for everybody anyway.

When Line Marcia appeared in the doorway in full mourning, looking very blonde and pale, a shiver ran through the crowd, as if a film star had come into view, and it seemed for a moment as if they were going to break into applause.

She got into a huge black car, which set off at a walking pace. The entire staff of La Sardine followed immediately behind, then came the old guard, men of Monsieur Maurice's age or even older. They walked along bare-headed with their hats in their hands, a picture of dignity, as people thronged the windows to get a look.

There was a certain elegance to it all in the glorious sunshine, and Marcia would have been happy with such a send-off.

When Maigret looked around, he saw that the procession, spanning the full width of the streets, was over three hundred metres long. Traffic had to be diverted by policemen with white batons, who were gesticulating feverishly.

'Hell of a funeral!' called a boy who was passing.

The church was already full, as predicted, except for the front few pews, which had been cordoned off with black ropes.

Line walked in alone, still at the head of the procession, perfectly straight-backed, her blue eyes impenetrable.

She went and sat in the first pew, still alone, while the restaurant's staff sat in the second. There were people standing in both naves and more outside, who couldn't get in. The great doors had been propped open, letting in the spring breeze.

The organ struck up a funeral march, and moments later the service began.

Standing in the left aisle, Maigret studied the mourners' faces and soon spotted Mori's. He had taken his place in the row of prominent figures and men of authority as if it was his by right, despite being the youngest.

His gaze met Maigret's. It quivered with a sort of defiance.

Maigret didn't wait for the end of the service. He was hot and thirsty. He went outside, then immediately ducked into the shade of a bar and ordered a glass of beer.

'That's some funeral,' muttered the owner who was very old and whose hand shook a little. 'Who is he, anyway?'

'The owner of La Sardine restaurant.'

'At the top of Rue Fontaine?'

'Yes.'

'I thought he was a gangster.'

'He was in his younger days.'

Maigret downed his beer in one, paid and went to find the Police Judiciaire's black car.

'The office.'

'Right, chief.'

It was eleven o'clock. Just time to grab his bag and shake Janvier's hand, and then Maigret was heading to Orly in the same car.

Were Line and Manuel going to travel together? Would the coffin be taken to Bandol by plane?

After completing the formalities, he still had a little time before boarding and went looking for the head of the airport police. He was an acquaintance from his days working at Quai des Orfèvres.

'Are you off to Bandol?'

Maigret had to control his temper.

'Yes. I think I'm leaving in about twenty minutes.'

'They'll be calling the passengers any moment.'

'Listen. Do you know if a plane has been chartered to carry a coffin?'

'Monsieur Maurice?'

'Yes.'

'He and his wife will be boarding a private plane that she has hired at around three o'clock – him in the pine box, her outside it, obviously.'

Maigret chose not to shrug.

'How long will the journey take them?'

'They're landing at Toulon, then a hearse will take the body from there to Bandol. It's only fourteen kilometres.'

'Passengers for Marseille,' the loudspeaker began.

Maigret headed to the designated gate. Ten minutes later, the plane, a twin-propellered aircraft, took off.

He had intended to enjoy the view because he was particularly fond of the country south of Lyon, but he didn't have a chance, falling asleep well before they flew over the Rhône. He took a cab from Marseille airport to the station and half an hour later caught a train to Bandol.

He felt a bit ridiculous, with his case propped on his knees and his hat, which he kept taking off to mop his brow.

When he stepped on to the platform at Bandol, the sun literally burned his skin, and he began to regret coming. Taxis were waiting outside the station as well as an old horse-drawn carriage, and Maigret chose the carriage.

'Where shall I take you, boss?'

'Do you know a good hotel by the sea?'

'I'll have you there in quarter of an hour.'

The wheels sank slightly into the tarmac, which had grown soft in the heat. The town was almost white, like Algiers, and palm trees lined some of the avenues.

He spied the sea, tricolour blue, through the greenery, and then the beach, where only a few people were sunbathing and a half dozen were swimming. The season hadn't started yet.

They passed the Casino, and then there was the hotel, which was also white, with an enormous terrace dotted with coloured parasols.

'Do you have a room?'

'For how long?'

'Just one night.'

'For one? Would you rather be facing the sea?'

He filled in the registration card.

'Room 233.'

The hotel was called the Tamarisks. It was cool and very clean.

'Can I get a drink?'

'The bar's at the end, on the right.'

He went in and drank a glass of beer.

'You're not Detective Chief Inspector Maigret, are you?' asked the barman after studying him for a moment.

He was a young man, very blond. His boldness had made him blush.

'Are you going to be on the Riviera for a long time?'

'Until tomorrow.'

'I thought so. You've come for Monsieur Maurice's burial, haven't you?'

'Is he very well known locally?'

'He was like God himself round here, put it like that.'

'Is his house far?'

'A good quarter of an hour's walk. It's almost at the other end of the front, not far from Raimu's villa when he was alive. You'll recognize it by the huge swimming pool.'

Maigret still had the feeling he was cheating, that he had sneaked off on an illicit holiday.

'What about the graveyard?'

'It's less than a kilometre from the villa. There's going to be a huge crowd, you know. They've been coming in from Toulon and Marseille since this morning.'

'What sort of people?'

'Big shots. I'm almost wondering whether the sub-prefect won't come. People are talking about it.'

Maigret drank another beer and, after checking his watch, slowly set off. Luckily the avenues along the sea-front were in the shade.

'I'll have to come here for a few days with my wife,' he thought.

The plane must have unloaded the coffin and Line at Toulon by now. The further he went, the more people he saw, and when he got to a corner he was greeted by almost the same sight as in Rue Ballu that morning.

How many of these people knew the truth? Not that it mattered, because none of them would talk.

Only one person had done that, from a telephone box, without even giving his name, and now he was hiding God knew where in Montmartre.

5.

He spotted a familiar face just on the edge of the crowd. It was Boutang, head of the Police Judiciaire in Toulon.

'Funny,' Boutang said, shaking his hand, 'I was thinking about you this morning as I was shaving. I had a feeling you'd come.'

He gestured to the crowd.

'What do you reckon? We could clean up here. It's not just the pick of Toulon's crooks who've come here, but also their counterparts in Marseille, Cannes and Nice.'

Someone came up to them, and Boutang shook his hand, made the introductions.

'Charmeroy, Bandol chief of police. I imagine you recognize Detective Chief Inspector Maigret, Charmeroy?'

'It's a great honour.'

They were sturdy characters. Men who knew their stuff and weren't easily intimidated.

'Nine-tenths of the people here live outside the law, and the amazing thing is that we can't prove anything against a single one of them.'

'When Marcia spent the summer in Bandol, did he have many guests?'

'Very few, actually. Some off his inner circle. Particularly the Mori brothers.'

'Did they stay at the house?'

'Yes. And, as luck would have it, it was always at the time of the big housebreaks. You must have read about them in the papers. Summer visitors with a huge villa on the Riviera and a yacht, who would set off on a cruise around the Greek islands in July or August, and then be stunned when they got back to find their furniture and valuables gone.'

'Same as the chateaus.'

'More or less. I suspected the Mori brothers and even the boss, the one they call Monsieur Maurice. I had the house watched. And, coincidentally enough, every time there was a robbery, the Moris didn't leave the house but played gin rummy with Marcia until the early hours . . . Do you know his wife? She's got class. You'd imagine she'd feel out of place in that world.'

The cortège arrived. Line was sitting alone in a car directly behind the hearse, followed by a throng of cars with Riviera number plates, mainly big American models, although there was also a smattering of sports cars for the younger generation.

All of them drove at a walking pace, as another crowd followed as best it could on foot. There was a moment of confusion. The hearse driver was about to turn right near the villa when the master of ceremonies ran up and gave him new instructions.

The two groups merged. Everyone seemed to know each other. Handshakes, whispered conversations.

Madame Marcia got out of her car and headed to the villa. She had changed since the morning. She was now wearing a thin black suit and a white silk hat. Her gloves were white too.

What was she going to do in the house on her own? Maigret couldn't think of a plausible answer to that question, nor could Boutang and the local police chief.

She was gone for less than ten minutes then got back in the car. The cortège did an about-turn, set off down Rue des Écoles, then Avenue du Onze-Novembre, and suddenly they were at the graveyard gates.

More confusion as people ran between the headstones to get a good spot near the graveside.

A priest was already in position and he greeted Line.

She showed no more sign of crying than she had that morning at the church of Notre-Dame-de-Lorette. The heavy coffin was lowered into the grave. The priest said a few prayers in a quiet voice, then the flowers, which had been stacked on the neighbouring graves in the meantime, were placed on the coffin.

'All the big underworld bosses are here. And all the young guns, who are proud to be seen with them. What are you going to do now, detective chief inspector?'

'I don't know yet.'

'Where are you staying?'

'The Tamarisks.'

'It's very good, and they're nice people, the owners.'

Line had already driven off to the house. Maigret hadn't spotted Manuel Mori or his brother in the crowd.

'I think I'll pay a visit.'

'Do you think she was in on it?'

'I don't think, I know. Trouble is, I haven't got any proof.'

'Good luck. If you need me, you know where to find me and where to find Charmeroy.'

The crowd was gradually breaking up and heading into town for a cold drink at one of the bars. Only a few cars, belonging to the real bigshots, had headed straight back to Toulon or Marseille.

Maigret found himself standing alone in front of the white villa. It wasn't overwhelmingly large. It was just a pretty villa, nothing more, and the most striking thing about it was the swimming pool surrounded by swing-seats. The garden consisted of a few palm trees, a mass of cacti and some tropical-looking plants which Maigret did not recognize.

He walked up the three steps to the front door, rang the electric bell and was surprised to see the door open instantly and Line standing there in front of him.

'I should have guessed you wouldn't stay away. You have no respect for mourning, do you?'

'Do you?'

The front door opened straight into a huge hall with white walls, where the furniture and decoration were as refined as those in the town-house in Rue Ballu, although of a different style.

She didn't ask him to sit down. She stood, waiting for him to speak. The hand holding her cigarette trembled a little.

'I'd like to talk to you about the night your husband died.'

'I thought I'd already answered your questions on that subject.'

'You didn't tell the truth, so now I'm going to ask you them again.'

Maigret sat down in one of the cream leather armchairs.

'You're only doing this because I'm not strong enough to throw you out.'

'You wouldn't dare anyway. If only to avoid implicating your lover.'

She turned pale with fury and went and stubbed out her cigarette in an ashtray.

'Don't you have any humanity?'

'I've got more than enough, as a matter of fact. But it depends who I'm talking to. You obviously married Marcia for his money.'

'That's my business.'

She sat down finally, crossed her legs and lit another cigarette which she had taken out of a gold box on a pedestal table.

'Manuel and you were in bed. Someone hammered on the door, and Mori, I suppose, put on a dressing gown while you hid under the sheets.'

She didn't flinch. Her face was impassive now. Her bright-blue eyes seemed devoid of almost anything except curiosity.

'And then?'

'It was your husband.'

'And what did he do, do you think? Did he shake Manuel's hand?'

'He took his gun out of his pocket.'

'Like in a movie.'

'What interests me is where Mori's gun was. In a drawer, obviously. But that could just as easily have been in the bedroom as in the drawing room.'

'You'd have to prove there was a gun in the apartment.'

She lit her cigarette.

'And that I was there. And that there was a visitor who happened to be none other than my husband. Not a very promising start, detective chief inspector.'

Maigret was about to reply when she said, barely raising her voice:

'Come in, darling.'

A door opened immediately, and Manuel appeared in shorts and espadrilles, as if he had come straight from the beach.

'We get around, detective chef inspector, don't we?'

He sardonically looked Maigret up and down, then went to the bar and poured himself a Tom Collins.

'Do you want one too, sweetheart?'

'I am quite thirsty, actually.'

'What about you, flatfoot?'

'No.'

'Suit yourself. No use showing me your little yellow form here. You're a long way from your stamping ground.'

'I could easily get a warrant.'

'But you won't.'

'Why not?'

'Because you haven't got anything on me.'

'Not even the Flea's testimony?'

'Have you found him?'

He was frowning.

'The Flea is the man, if that's the word for it, who knows the ninth and tenth arrondissements better than anyone, there's no doubt about that. He's also someone who people know, and most of them are willing to give him a helping hand. You're not going to find him, detective chief inspector. My men will. But you won't be able to prove that either . . . You see, I'm putting my cards on the table.

'If there were witnesses here, I'd swear, as I have already done, that I didn't fire a shot, that there weren't any shots fired in my apartment, and that Maurice wasn't there that night.

'Line and I would also repeat that there's never been anything between us, and I defy you to produce anyone in court who will claim otherwise.'

He wasn't putting it on. He was fired up, and Maigret wondered anxiously why he was so confident. He didn't seem to be afraid of anything any more, and Line was as calm as if there had never been such a person as Marcia.

Maigret immediately thought of the Flea. Had Mori's men, as he called them, finally got their hands on the midget? Had they seen to it that he would no longer be a threat, that he'd keep quiet for good?

Maigret filled his pipe, lit it, stood up and started pacing around the room.

'It's true that I'm outside my jurisdiction here, so I can't use the documents I showed you in Paris.'

'Exactly.'

'But it would only take a telephone call for Detective Chief Inspector Boutang to be here with a search warrant in half an hour at the most. I suppose you know Boutang?'

'He's not a friend.'

'So, it's up to you. Either you show me round the villa or I ring Toulon.'

'Be my guest, have a look around. Just don't take anything.'

Maigret made a discovery in the big drawing room itself. One of the walls was taken up by a bookcase full of expensively bound books, like in Paris.

On the lower shelves, there were piles of magazines. They weren't the sort of weeklies you'd find on regular newsstands, and they didn't go with Monsieur Maurice's character either. Maigret read out their titles under his breath, checking that they had at least been leafed through.

'*Farms and Chateaus.* That's a very enlightening read, isn't it? *Country Life. Art and Decoration . . .*'

Mori frowned and glanced at his mistress.

'They're mine,' she said. 'I don't play cards, so when the men have a game of gin rummy I sit in the corner and read.'

The next room was an old dining room in the Provençal style, with a boudoir off to the left, in which every object and piece of furniture could have been in a museum, again like in Paris.

'Is that genuine?' asked Maigret, pointing to a Van Gogh.

'I'm not an expert,' the woman replied, 'but my husband wasn't in the habit of buying fakes.'

The kitchen was huge, modern, spotless.

'You don't entertain much, though.'

'How do you know that?'

'I've had time to make some inquiries. I also know that the Mori brothers used to stay with you for on average a month a year.'

'They were my husband's best friends.'

'Your husband who presumably had no inkling of your affair with Manuel . . .'

Manuel, who was following Maigret without a word, didn't flinch.

'You've got the wrong idea. My husband was sixty-two and had led a very full life. He was worn out, in a way. He might have been in love with me when he married me five years ago, but we soon started living like brother and sister.'

'Fine, go on lying. It doesn't bother me.'

He went up a marble staircase and pushed open a set of double doors that gave on to a vast bedroom with a terrace looking over the sea.

'Yours?'

There were twin beds, more exquisite furniture.

The bathroom was bigger than the one in Rue Ballu and lined throughout in pale-yellow marble.

'Only one bathroom for the two of you? That doesn't fit with your brother and sister story.'

'Think what you like.'

There were two other bedrooms upstairs, each with its own bathroom.

'For the Mori brothers, I suppose?'

'Guest rooms.'

'Did many guests use these rooms apart from them?'

'Now and then.'

The paintings were almost all old, by artists Maigret didn't know.

'Is there a loft?'

'No. There are attic rooms, where the staff sleep.'

'Are they here now?'

'No. I'm leaving this evening. A cleaner can manage the house by herself.'

'And you don't always rehire the same staff every year, is that right?'

'We do change them sometimes, yes.'

'So that for most of the year this house is empty at night, with no one to keep an eye on it.'

She nodded. Then he asked ironically:

'Aren't you afraid of burglars?'

'They wouldn't dare try to rob my husband's house.'

'Or yours, now you've inherited it.'

When they returned to the drawing room, rather than heading for the front door, Maigret went and sat in the armchair he had been sitting in before.

The couple exchanged looks.

'Can I remind you that our plane is waiting for us at Toulon.'

'*Your* plane. You used the plural. Does that mean Mori is travelling with you?'

'Why shouldn't he?'

'As a friend. All above board.'

'Actually,' Line put in, 'maybe it is time for a change of tune. You're right, we are lovers . . .'

'That's better.'

'It's nothing to make a fuss about.'

'Except when the husband gets a high-calibre bullet in the chest.'

He turned to Mori.

'We didn't finish our little conversation about that just now. We'd got to the point where you'd hurriedly pulled on a dressing gown and were heading for the front door. You opened it, naturally . . .'

'And . . .?'

'I'm waiting for you to tell me what happened next. Maurice Marcia didn't just stand there on the doorstep.'

'Did I say it was him?'

'Let's say you didn't deny it. He didn't settle down in the drawing room for a chat either. No, he walked straight through it to get to the bedroom. He just had to pull back the sheet to find his wife as naked as the day she was born . . .'

'So tactful!' sneered Line.

'In fact, he knew what he was going to find the moment he walked in. He knew it when he left La Sardine . . .'

'He'd known it for three years.'

'No. You're not going to convince me he was an accommodating husband, or that he was impotent. He was probably holding his gun. Mori, you had your pistol in the pocket of your dressing gown. Where had you got it from?'

'I didn't have a gun of any sort in the apartment.'

'Who pulled the trigger then? Marcia's automatic wasn't fired. And the gun that killed him is probably somewhere at the bottom of the Seine.'

'Send divers down to look for it, then.'

Maigret pursued his train of thought undeterred.

'Let's suppose you went to open the door unarmed, which is possible . . .'

'Finally!'

'I haven't finished . . . You grabbed a gun when you saw Marcia heading for the bedroom . . . Unless the gun was in the drawer of the bedside table and a kind soul passed it to you to defend yourself . . .'

'I'd like to hear this story in front of a jury.'

'There's another possibility.'

'What is it? I'm on tenterhooks.'

'That you weren't the one who killed—'

'Oh look, another character comes on stage to play the crook.'

'No. Line has all the time in the world, while you go and open the door, to get the gun that was in the bedside table. And when Marcia threatened you, she . . .'

'She'd have definitely hit the ceiling because she's never used a firearm in her life.'

'We'll discuss this later.'

'In Paris, fine.'

'In my office, this time.'

'Why not?'

'You might leave in handcuffs.'

'It's not very classy trying to scare me. What if I left the country first?'

'Interpol would soon find you. You're forgetting you've got a record and, besides, you're pretty flashy.

'I imagine you two are planning to get married after a suitable interval?'

'Stranger things have happened.'

'There's a plane waiting for you.'

'Don't you want a seat?' Manuel jeered.

Maigret looked at him with the calm he had displayed all afternoon, the sort that comes before a storm.

He ate bouillabaisse in a spick and span little restaurant, sitting off on his own in a corner. He didn't get as much enjoyment from it as he had hoped, which must have been down to his state of mind.

Night had fallen. The tree-lined walks facing the sea were softly lit and he could hear the faint murmur of the waves.

He sat down on a bench. The air was soft. He felt lazy. If he had had his way, he would have sent for Madame Maigret, and they would have had a week's holiday in Bandol.

He quickly went to bed and fell asleep immediately. The next day he had to get up early to catch his flight from Marseille and he landed at Orly at 10.30.

He took a taxi and had it drop him off at home first. His wife didn't greet him effusively, but it was obvious from her beaming smile that it had done her the world of good seeing him again.

'Not too tired?'

'A little.'

'Shall I make you a cup of coffee?'

'No thanks. I have to look in at the office.'

'Still this wretched case?'

'This wretched case, exactly.'

'They were talking about you in the evening papers

yesterday. They say you're being mysterious, that you're worried – demoralized, even – and that you're definitely hiding something.'

'If they only knew! I don't know if I'll be able to come back for lunch. It'll depend on what's waiting for me at the office. By the way, one of these days we'll have to go to Bandol.'

He went back out to the little car waiting by the kerb and moments later was climbing the large staircase at Quai des Orfèvres. Paperwork, reports and a few letters were already piling up on his desk. He went to open the door of the inspectors' office and called Janvier in.

'Good trip, chief?'

'Not bad. Guess who was in the villa even before Madame Marcia?'

'Mori, obviously.'

'Right. He's a tough nut, I tell you. He's going to make life harder for us before he comes clean . . .'

'I've got some good news for you. Well, semi-good news. Inspector Louis rang this morning. He missed the Flea by a few hours and wants to talk to you. He'll be in his office all morning so you can call him.'

'Do it for me, will you? Tell him I'll come and see him.'

He went and stood by the open window, as delighted to rediscover 'his' view of the Seine as if he'd been gone for weeks. It was sultry. A storm was brewing but it probably wouldn't break before evening.

'He's waiting for you.'

'Are you coming? That'll give us a chance to talk on the way.'

As they drove, Maigret filled Janvier in on what had happened in Bandol. They stopped for a moment outside the police station on Place Saint-Georges, and Monsieur Louis, as some people solemnly called him to tease him, quickly got in.

'Do you want to see the last place he hid?'

'Yes.'

'Then stop right at the top of the hill, Place du Tertre.'

The pavements were lined with painters, and the little tables with red-checked tablecloths were ready for the tourists.

'Turn into Rue du Mont-Cenis and park by the kerb.'

Lower down the street there were newish apartment blocks but at the top most of the buildings still had an old-fashioned look. Inspector Louis led them down an alley between two houses, and they saw a glass-fronted studio at the end.

Louis knocked. A loud voice yelled:

'Come in!'

They found themselves in a sculptor's studio. The owner looked at Maigret through half-closed eyes, as he would have at a model.

'You're . . . you're Detective Chief Inspector Maigret, if I'm not mistaken?'

'You're not.'

'And he . . .'

'Inspector Janvier.'

'It's been years since I've had this many people in my studio.'

He had white hair, a matching goatee and moustache, and rosy cheeks, like a baby's.

'Monsieur Sorel is the oldest artist in Montmartre,' explained Inspector Louis. 'How long did you say you've been in this studio?'

'Fifty-three years. I've seen painters come and go, starting with Picasso, who I often ate with.'

He had a slightly naive, childlike expression. A look around his studio dispelled any illusions about his talent. He only sculpted children's heads – or rather, what looked like the same child's head, with different expressions – and presumably then sold his busts at the art dealer's on Place du Tertre.

'Apparently you had the Flea to stay?'

'For a couple of days and nights. He left yesterday evening after dark. He doesn't dare stay longer in one place in case he's spotted.'

'How did he come to choose your studio?'

'Suppose I were to tell you that I met him when he was barely fifteen? Back then he was a street kid, who got by however he could and often went hungry.

'Seeing him one day on Place du Tertre, I asked him if he wanted to pose for me, and he came around. I remember the bust I did of him, one of my best, which is now in some collection or other. With his grimacing face and huge mouth, I created a more lifelike clown than I ever would have if I'd had a professional as a model.

'He was a good little boy. Now and then he'd come and knock on my door, especially in winter, and ask if he could sleep on the straw mattress. It was my dog's mattress, because I had a dog in those days, a big St Bernard, but that's another story.'

'Did he tell you about his troubles?'

'He asked if I could hide him for a night or two. I asked if he was on the run from the police. He said it was the other way around; he was on very good terms with Inspector Louis and Detective Chief Inspector Maigret. That was why certain people were after him.'

'When he left, did he tell you where he was going?'

'No. As far as I could gather, it wasn't a long way away. I get the impression he doesn't want to leave the neighbourhood.'

'Did he talk about anyone in particular in the last two days?'

'Yes. An ex-policeman who's retired now, who was kind to him when he was a kid. I don't know his name. I don't know him either. I only venture out of the studio to do my shopping, less than a hundred metres from here, and take my pieces to my dealer.'

It was only now that he seemed to realize that they were all standing.

'Sorry not to ask if you'd like to sit down but I don't have enough chairs or stools. As for offering you a drink, I've only got cheap red, the sort Utrillo drank, which you'll probably find too rough.'

'Did he go anywhere in those two days and nights?'

'No. But he was surprised and very pleased to find out that I had a telephone. He rang a woman to let her know how he was, and I discreetly went out into the courtyard to smoke a pipe.

'All I can tell you is that he was very frightened. He couldn't keep still. He started at every sound and asked me at least ten times if anyone ever came to see me . . . Who'd come and see me? . . . I don't even want a cleaning lady!'

Maigret looked at him affectionately; there were very few examples of old Montmartre like him still surviving.

'Wait a minute! He talked about you. Apparently you're meant to arrest someone, but he doesn't understand why you're taking so long.

' "If the detective chief inspector doesn't get a move on, he won't have anyone left to testify, because they'll kill me first." '

As he left after shaking the old man's hand, Maigret muttered to himself:

'A retired police officer . . .'

'I'm already following up that angle,' said Inspector Louis with his usual impassivity. 'It's likely to be an officer from the eighteenth arrondissement, or maybe the ninth, because he wouldn't have moved far when he stopped working. Those also seem to be the parts of town the Flea hung around in most when he was young.

'I've started working through the lists of policemen who have retired in the last ten years. I haven't found any with Montmartre addresses so far but I'll carry on this afternoon.'

In a neighbourhood where everyone knew each other, it would obviously have been easier to ask the first old lady who came along or the grocer, but wouldn't that be dangerous for the Flea?

'Where do you want us to drop you?'

'Nowhere. I'll stay around here.'

He had his methods. He was a sort of bloodhound and he would have been unhappy having to work in a team. No doubt he was going to do the rounds of the local bars again, drowning in glasses of Vichy as he listened to the conversations around him.

'Blanche Pigoud's house, Rue Fromentin.'

Maigret was beginning to worry about the Flea's fate too, but it wouldn't have done any good sending ten or twenty men out to look for him.

'By the way, are we still watching the Mori brothers?'

'The inspectors are working in shifts. While his brother was away, Jo spent a fair while in Rue du Caire, then drove off in the lorry and came back with it empty at about eight in the evening. He locked the metal shutter and went home to have a shower and change . . . Do you know where he had dinner?'

'Yes. La Sardine.'

'How did you guess?'

'Because they've already taken it over, in a way.'

'What about Manuel?'

'That's even easier. He had dinner at La Sardine too, with Line, which is probably the first time she's eaten at her husband's restaurant. Poor Marcia didn't know she'd soon be the owner.'

'This all smacks of defiance. The staff must have been outraged to see her with the Mori brothers on the day of the funeral.'

'Manuel doesn't give a damn what the staff think. If any

of them leaves, he'll replace them with his people. That's probably his plan, in fact. I bet he spent the night at Rue Ballu . . .'

'Right again. For all I know, he's still there.'

'There's a weak spot somewhere, though,' Maigret thought aloud.

'The Flea?'

'The Flea's no use to us until we get our hands on him. No, there's a weak spot somewhere else, and I'm getting a headache thinking about it.'

'Shall I come up with you?'

'It might be better if you didn't. Despite her profession, this girl is quite sensitive. She's used to me, but if we both show up . . .'

This time the Flea's young girlfriend was up and having her breakfast by the window.

'Cup of coffee? I've just made some.'

'In that case, yes, please.'

She seemed worried.

'Have you heard from him, inspector?'

'I know where he spent the last two nights, but he moved on yesterday evening.'

'What part of town was it?'

'Near Place du Tertre, at an old sculptor's.'

'That's funny. He told me about him once when we went to eat at the foot of Sacré-Coeur. It reminded him of his childhood round there. He described the straw mattress he sometimes slept on which was normally a big dog's bed.'

'Did he talk to you about anyone else who lived in the neighbourhood?'

'I don't remember. I don't think so.'

'A former policeman, say?'

'Honestly, that doesn't ring a bell.'

'Did he call you?'

'Twice.'

'What did he say?'

'He's getting more and more scared. He doesn't understand why you don't just arrest the Mori brothers. Their gang would quieten down, and Justin could breathe freely.'

'Is he angry with me?'

'A bit, I think, yes. He's angry with Inspector Louis too. I told him what you'd told me.'

'Listen. There's every chance he'll call you again, unless there isn't a telephone where he is. Tell him to call me. I'll give him all the assurances he wants.'

'Really?'

'I need to have a conversation with him and I wouldn't be surprised if two hours after that the Mori brothers weren't behind bars.'

'I'll tell him. I'll do all I can. Put yourself in his shoes, though. He doesn't trust anything, or anyone, any more.'

A quarter of an hour later, Maigret and Janvier were sitting at the bar in La Sardine. It was when they laid the tables for lunch, and the head waiter was on the telephone by the till, taking reservations.

'A glass of beer, Freddy.'

'What about you?' the latter asked Janvier.

'I'll have the same.'

'We've only got foreign beer left.'

'That's all right.'

There was something grudging about the way Freddy served them, and he kept glancing at the door as if he was afraid one of the Mori brothers was about to walk in.

'I've never seen so many people at a funeral,' Maigret said, trying to draw him out.

'There were a lot of people, yes.'

'It was almost as packed in Bandol. People came from all over, Nice, Cannes, Toulon, Marseille. And the cars! I counted at least five Ferraris.'

Freddy imperturbably wiped the glasses. Comitat, the head waiter, had finished speaking on the telephone but, rather than come over to them, remained on the other side of the restaurant, apparently ignoring them.

'Bit cool today,' Maigret joked.

The thermometer must have read twenty-five degrees in the shade.

'Yes, it is a bit cool.'

'So have you finally seen your boss, then?'

'What boss?'

'Line Marcia. She ate here last night with the Mori brothers. Although it's Manuel who's really the boss.'

'Listen, Monsieur Maigret. I don't get involved in your business, so don't you get involved in what's going on here. For a start, if anyone saw me chatting to you, it could be bad for me. It might not be so good for you either.'

Maigret and Janvier exchanged glances.

'Wait a minute, will you, Janvier?'

He set off for the lavatory, which took him past Comitat.

'Hello, Monsieur Raoul,' he called out.

'Freddy must have told you that you're not welcome here.'

'He did. Change of owner. Now everyone seems on edge.'

'I'd be obliged if you didn't come back.'

'You're forgetting this is a public place, open to anyone who is decently dressed and has a relatively healthy bank balance.'

He went to the lavatory, then back to the bar. It was just after 12.15.

'You know what we're going to do, Janvier? We're going to have lunch here.'

They headed towards the nearest table. Comitat came rushing over.

'I'm sorry but that table's taken.'

'We'll have the one next to it, then.'

'It's taken too. All the tables are taken.'

'Well, in that case, let's say this one is taken by me. Have a seat, Janvier.'

Maigret wasn't being childish. He was furious and he wanted them to be too.

'Bring me the menu, please. And don't forget that I can have this place shut down in twenty-four hours.'

The menu was enormous, with a wine list on the back.

'They've got scallops, Janvier. What do you think?'

'I like the sound of those.'

'Then braised rib of beef.'

'And that.'

He gave back the menu.

'Let's have a light wine. A Beaujolais?'

'Good idea.'

The head waiter stood behind them, ramrod straight, until four customers came in and sat at a table by the window. The small brown-haired cashier had taken up her post, but Maigret's attempts to say hello were unsuccessful. She didn't seem to recognize him.

Monsieur Maurice was dead. When he was alive no one talked out of turn, but even so the restaurant had a relatively easy-going atmosphere.

Then Mori had shown up yesterday evening with Madame Marcia to take over, and everyone had got the message.

From now on they were going to have to watch their step. They had already started. At most they managed to stammer a few words as they squeezed past each other.

'What do you bet we won't be served for half an hour, if not an hour?'

Sure enough, the table of four was served before them, then two Englishmen who had only just come in. The restaurant gradually filled up, and the longer it took for them to be served, the more Maigret smiled and pointedly smoked his pipe.

'Don't rush,' he said as the head waiter passed their table.

'No, monsieur, I don't intend to.'

The Moris didn't appear, and the two men were eventually given something to eat and drink.

6.

It was after three when Maigret got back to Quai des Orfèvres, and the first person he saw was the inexhaustible Inspector Louis, sitting on one of the benches in the corridor, his black hat on his knees.

Maigret showed him into his office, and Louis again perched on the edge of a chair.

'I think I've had a stroke of luck, sir.'

He had the soft voice of a shy person and rarely looked people he was talking to in the face.

'When I left you this morning, I started on another round of the bars and cafés at the top of Montmartre, around Place du Tertre. I know, it's a compulsion of mine . . . I got to the Trois Tonneaux, a popular bistro in Rue Gabrielle. I stood at the bar, as always, and had my usual small bottle of Vichy.'

Maigret knew it was no use hurrying him. The inspector spoke with the deliberation and attention to detail that were part of his character.

'In one corner, under a promotional clock, four men were playing belote. They were all getting on and had probably been playing their game at the same time and the same table for years . . .

'I jumped when I heard one of them say:

' "Your turn, sergeant."

'The man he was talking to must have been seventy or seventy-five, but he was still sprightly.

'Three times in the space of ten minutes someone called him sergeant when they spoke to him.

' "Is he a policeman?" I asked the owner quietly.

' "He was for forty years. Talk about an officer of the old school. Everyone knew him around the neighbourhood. He was like a father to all the kids."

' "Has he been retired for long?"

' "At least ten years. He comes and plays his card game every day. He lives alone now his son has got married and moved to Meaux. His daughter is a nurse at Bichat hospital, and he's got another son who does something or other – gets up to no good, I imagine."

' "Does he live nearby?"

' "Not very far. Rue Tholozé. Just opposite the only dance hall in the street. His wife died five years ago, and he does his own cooking and cleaning. We get a lot of his kind round here, little old men and women living alone on a modest pension.'

Maigret knew Montmartre well enough to know it was a city within a city. Some people never ventured below Place Clichy.

'Did you get his exact address?'

'I left the bistro so as not to attract attention. The man came out half an hour later and stopped at the butcher's to buy a couple of chops.

'Keeping my distance, because he must know all about tailing someone, I followed him to Rue Tholozé. He went into a three-storey building directly opposite the

Tam-Tam, a music hall. I rang the eighteenth arrondisse-ment station to ask for a detective's assistance for an hour or two. One of them came, a young fellow, and he's keep-ing watch not far from the building.'

With that, he fell silent. He had said all he had to, in his own way.

'Did you hear that, Janvier?'

Janvier had come into the office at the same time as Maigret.

'Are we off?'

'Of course.'

'Shall we take some men?'

'No need. We have to be as discreet as possible.'

They took one of the small black cars parked in the Police Judiciaire's courtyard.

'Isn't Rue Tholozé a one-way street?'

'It must be, there are stairs at the other end.'

As they pulled into the street, they saw the young policeman standing some way from the building.

'I'll go in on my own,' said Maigret. 'There's no point scaring him.'

He spoke to the concierge, showing his policeman's badge.

'Is the sergeant at home?'

'Monsieur Colson? That's right, everybody still calls him the sergeant. He got back about two hours ago. He's probably taking a nap now.'

'What floor?'

'Third, left-hand door.'

Naturally there was no lift. The building was old, like

almost all the buildings in the street, and there was a strong smell of cooking on the stairs.

No sign of a doorbell. Maigret knocked.

'Come in,' said a deep voice.

The apartment was small and cluttered with what had once been the furniture for a whole house. In the bedroom off to the right there were two beds, one of which looked as if it had been used by a series of children.

Everything was in duplicate or triplicate. Rather than a refrigerator, there was a wire-netting meat safe hanging out of the window.

'I don't believe it! Detective Chief Inspector Maigret in my home! Come in, please. Someone's going to be very pleased.'

He showed Maigret into a stifling room that doubled as a dining and living room. A man under one metre fifty tall, who looked like a child with a freakishly wrinkled face, was staring anxiously at the visitor.

'Have you arrested him?' he blurted out immediately.

'Not yet, but you're not in any danger.'

'I told him at least ten times that he should call you and tell you where he is,' Sergeant Colson put in. 'He was shaking all over when he got here. He's terrified of these Mori brothers . . . That's their name, isn't it? We hadn't heard of them in my time.'

'They're barely in their thirties.'

'I watch television in the evenings but I don't read the papers. Justin remembered me. I knew him when he used to hang around the neighbourhood and wear just a pair of old espadrilles.'

'What are you going to do with me?'

The Flea was tense and couldn't relax.

'The two of us are going to go to Quai des Orfèvres, where we'll have a private conversation in my office, and after we've talked, chances are the Mori brothers will be arrested.'

'How did you find me?'

'Inspector Louis picked up your trail.'

'They could have too.'

'Thank you for taking him in, sergeant. I hope the chops were good.'

'How do you know . . .?'

'Inspector Louis again. And have a good game of belote tomorrow morning!'

He turned to the midget, who still hadn't relaxed.

'Come on, you.'

The retired sergeant showed them to the door and watched a little sadly as they went down the stairs.

'Get in the car.'

The Flea found himself sitting in the back with Inspector Louis.

'There I was, thinking I had such a good hiding place,' Justin sighed.

'It was pure luck I picked up the sergeant's trail.'

He sat as far from the door as he could for fear of being seen from outside. They went up the Police Judiciaire's stairs together, the Flea looking around him with a sort of fearful respect. Maigret couldn't decide whether to show all three of them into his office or question Justin Crotton on his own.

He decided on the latter approach.

'I'll see you both in a minute,' he told Louis and Janvier. 'Come in . . .'

He almost said 'kid' but caught himself in time.

'Have a seat. Do you smoke?'

'Yes.'

'Do you have any cigarettes?'

'I've got two left.'

'Have this packet.'

Maigret always had two or three packets of cigarettes in his drawer for whoever he might be talking to.

'What do you . . .'

'One moment.'

There was a note on his desk. 'The laboratory would like you to call them.'

He asked the switchboard to put him through to Moers.

'Have you got something?'

'Yes. The laboratory's done a good job. The textile man has been to see the leading carpet dealer in Paris, and his first impressions have been confirmed. The silk threads are from an old Chinese rug; it must be sixteenth or seventeenth century. Other than in museums, there can't be more than three or four like it in France.

'The dealer doesn't know who they belong to. He's going to make inquiries. There's something else more important, though. There were minute traces of blood on the carpet under the rug. It was very diluted with water. The stain must have been repeatedly gone over with a scrubbing brush, because they also found bristles.'

'Is it possible to tell what group the blood is from?'

'We already have. It's AB.'

'No one thought to test Monsieur Maurice's blood before it was too late, unfortunately. Unless the pathologist . . .'

'Yes. He might have. Have you got his report?'

'He doesn't mention it.'

The Flea was looking at Maigret as if he still couldn't believe what was happening to him. But why couldn't he relax? What was he still afraid of?

Maigret went and opened the door.

'Janvier, try to get hold of the pathologist as quickly as possible. Ask him if it occurred to him to analyse Marcia's blood. If it didn't, find out what's happened to the clothes.'

Twenty or so inspectors were typing up reports and, in the middle of them, Louis was sitting bolt upright on a chair, his hat on his knees.

Going back into his office, Maigret said to the Flea:

'Let's see. What time is it? Four o'clock. Chances are we'll find your girlfriend still at home.'

Sure enough, Blanche Pigoud's was the voice he heard on the other end of the telephone.

'Is that you, Justin?'

'No, it's Detective Chief Inspector Maigret here.'

'Have you heard anything?'

'He's in my office.'

'Did he turn himself in?'

'No. We had to go and fetch him.'

'Where was he?'

'In Montmartre, as I expected.'

'Have you arrested the . . .'

'The Mori brothers. No. One thing at a time. Here's Justin.'

He motioned to him to take the telephone.

'Hello? Is that you?'

He was very awkward, overawed.

'I don't know yet . . . I've hardly been here a quarter of an hour, and no one's asked me anything. I'm well, yes . . . No . . . I don't know when I'll be back . . . Goodbye.'

'You won't have much longer to wait before you see him,' said Maigret, after the Flea passed him the receiver. 'You'll feel reassured now, at least.'

He hung up, slowly lit his pipe and studied Justin Crotton carefully. He couldn't understand why he was still so on edge.

'Do you always tremble like that?'

'No.'

'What are you afraid of right now, here, in my office? Me?'

'Maybe.'

'Why?'

'Because you scare me. Everything to do with the police scares me.'

'But as a last resort you took refuge with a former police sergeant.'

'I don't think of Sergeant Colson as a real policeman. I've known him since I was barely sixteen, and it's thanks to him that I've never been convicted of vagrancy.'

'On the other hand, I . . .?'

'You're so high up.'

'How did you know that Line Marcia was Manuel's mistress?'

'Everyone in the clubs knew.'

'But Monsieur Maurice was in the dark about it for three years?'

'Seems so.'

'You're not sure?'

'It's always the one who's most involved who finds out last, isn't it? Monsieur Maurice was a rich, influential man. I don't think anyone would have dared go up to him and say to his face:

'"Your wife is cheating on you with one of your friends."'

'Marcia and the Mori brothers were friends?'

'Had been for a few years, yes.'

'How do you know?'

'Because the Mori brothers were regulars at La Sardine, and Monsieur Maurice would come and sit at their table. They'd sometimes stay after closing.'

'Did they go to Rue Ballu too?'

'I saw them go into the building several times.'

'When Marcia was at home?'

'Yes.'

'How do you know all this?'

'Because I poke around all over the place. I've got big ears. I listen to what people are saying. They trust me.'

'Do you often go to La Sardine?'

'The bar, yes. Freddy's a friend, almost.'

'I doubt he is any more.'

'On the night of the murder I was in Rue Fontaine when Monsieur Maurice came rushing out at a very unusual time for him.'

'When?'

'Just after midnight. He didn't take his car but walked off very fast towards Square La Bruyère.'

'Did you know his wife was in Manuel's apartment?'

'Yes.'

'How did you know she was there that particular evening?'

'Because I'd followed her.'

'So, you're obsessed with watching people and following them, is that right?'

'I always dreamed of becoming a policeman. They wouldn't let me because of my height. Maybe my lack of schooling too.'

'Right . . . So, you're following Monsieur Maurice . . . He goes into Manuel's . . . Were there lights on in the windows?'

'Yes.'

'How long had Line been there?'

'An hour, maybe.'

'Did you go into the building?'

'No.'

'Did you guess what was going to happen?'

'Yes. Except that I didn't know which of them would be killed.'

'Did you hear the shot?'

'No. The people living in the building didn't either, or else they thought it was a car backfiring.'

'Go on.'

'After about a quarter of an hour, Madame Marcia came out of the building and hurried home.'

'Did you follow her?'

'No, I thought I'd wait.'

'What happened after that?'

'A car came speeding up, and I was almost caught. It was the other Mori, Jo. His brother must have rung him and asked him to drop everything and come over.'

Maigret was following this account with increasing interest. He hadn't spotted any obvious flaw in it but he still felt a vague sense of unease.

'Then what?'

'The two men came out carrying a rolled-up rug with something heavy inside.'

'Marcia's body?'

'Almost definitely. They hoisted the bundle into the car and drove off towards Place Constantin-Pecqueur. I didn't have a car so I couldn't follow them.'

'What did you do?'

'I stayed there, waiting.'

'Were they gone for a long time?'

'Nearly half an hour.'

'Did they bring the rug back?'

'No. I didn't see it again. They both went up to the apartment, and Jo only came out an hour later.'

That all held water. The two men had probably taken the body to the darkest part of Avenue Junot first and then thrown the rug into the Seine.

When they got back to Square La Bruyère, they would then have carefully covered up any trace of what had happened.

'What did you do after that?'

'I waited until morning before ringing Inspector Louis.'

'Why him and not the police station, say, or the Police Judiciaire?'

'Because they scare me.'

And he was genuinely scared.

'This wasn't the first time you'd called him, was it?'

'No. I've been feeding him information like that for a long time. I know him by sight. We go to pretty much the same places. He's always on his own.'

'Why did you disappear?'

'Because I guessed the Mori brothers would realize it was me.'

Maigret frowned. This was the least convincing part of his statement.

'Why would they think it was you? Had you talked to them?'

'No. But they'd seen me in bars. They know that I roam around all over Montmartre and that I'm well informed . . .'

'No,' Maigret snapped.

The Flea looked at him bewildered, then afraid.

'What do you mean?'

'It would have taken more than that for them to decide to kill you.'

'I swear . . .'

'Didn't you ever speak to them?'

'Never. Just ask them.'

Maigret sensed he was lying but couldn't prove it.

'All right, we'll arrest them. In the meantime, come into the next-door office with me . . . Wait quietly in here. One of the inspectors may have a newspaper he can lend you.'

'I don't like reading.'

'Fine . . . Don't work yourself into a state.'

Maigret motioned to Janvier to follow him into his office.

'Have you spoken to the Forensic Institute?'

'I got Doctor Bourdet himself on the telephone. The clothes and underwear are still there. The blood group is AB.'

'Same as the blood found on the rug.'

'Apparently it's the most common group in the country.'

'I'm going up to see the examining magistrate and then I'll probably need you and Lucas. Lapointe too.'

Maigret walked down the long corridor containing the examining magistrates' offices. The benches against the walls were almost all occupied by people waiting to appear before them. Some were in handcuffs, with gendarmes either side, while others, with less glassy expressions, were only witnesses, or accused but not in custody.

Maigret knocked on Bouteille's door, went in and found the examining magistrate dictating to his clerk.

'Excuse me.'

'Have a seat. It's just red tape, as usual. Have you used the warrants?'

'Only the search warrant. An old Chinese rug has gone missing from the older Mori brother's bedroom. The carpet underneath had a few stains which have proved to be bloodstains. Group AB. Marcia's clothes, which Doctor Bourdet has examined, have the same type of blood where he was shot.'

'That's not proof, as you know.'

'It's a clue. Others are that Mori slept at Rue Ballu the night of the funeral, and that the two brothers have pretty much taken over La Sardine.'

'Have you found that little midget? What's his nickname again?'

'The Flea. He's downstairs, under guard. He confirms that shortly after midnight he saw Monsieur Maurice enter the apartment building on Square La Bruyère where the older Mori lives. A quarter of an hour later, Line Marcia came out and walked quickly off in the direction of her home. Finally the younger Mori drove up, as if he'd been called in as back-up by telephone.

'Half an hour later, the two brothers came down, carrying a heavy bundle which they hoisted into the car.

'The Flea couldn't follow them to Avenue Junot as he didn't have a car but he is positive. The body was wrapped in a multicoloured rug.'

'Are you planning to arrest them?'

'This afternoon. But I'd like another warrant, this time for Madame Line Marcia.'

'Do you think she . . .?'

'She's certainly complicit. I suspect she handed the gun to her lover. I almost wonder whether she didn't fire it.'

The examining magistrate turned to his clerk.

'You heard. Draw up the warrant . . . I get the impression they'll be hard nuts to crack.'

'I do too. And it would be reckless taking them to court without solid proof because they'll not only hire the best lawyers in Paris but they'll also have all the false witnesses they could wish for.'

Soon afterwards, Maigret returned to his office and did something unusual: he took his gun out of a drawer and slipped it into his pocket. Then he called in Lucas, Janvier and Lapointe.

'Come in, boys. This time we're going for broke. You're coming with me, Janvier. Go and get your gun, because we have to be prepared for anything with these people.

'You two do the same,' he told Lucas and Lapointe. 'You're going to Rue du Caire, where you'll probably find the younger Mori brother. If not, try where he lives, the Hôtel des Iles in Avenue Trudaine. Finally, if he's not there either, try La Sardine. Here's the warrant you need for him. Take a pair of handcuffs while you're at it. You too, Janvier.'

They split up in the courtyard, and the two cars headed for their respective destinations.

'Where are we going?'

'To Manuel's first.'

The concierge told them that he was unlikely to be there but that the cleaning lady definitely was. They went up. The cleaning lady was terrifyingly thin, and they wondered how she could stay upright. She was in her sixties and must have been ill. The expression on her face was bitter, aggressive.

'What do you want?'

'Monsieur Manuel Mori.'

'He's not here.'

'What time did he go out?'

'I've no idea.'

'Did he sleep in his bed?'

'That's none of your business.'

'We're the police.'

'Police or no police, it's none of your business which bed a man sleeps in.'

'Have you noticed that the rug in the bedroom has disappeared?'

'So? If he burned a hole in it with a cigarette and sent it to be repaired, that's his business.'

'Is your boss pleasant to you?'

'Like a slap in the face.'

Employer and employee were cut from the same cloth.

'Well, are you just going to stand there? I'm going to get on with my vacuuming, because I haven't got time to waste.'

A few minutes later the two men pulled up outside what had been Marcia's home.

'Is Madame Marcia upstairs?' Maigret asked the concierge.

'I don't think she's gone out. Although you can always use the garden door, which is left open.'

'Day and night?'

'Yes.'

'So you don't know who comes in and out?'

'Not many people in the building use that door.'

'I get the impression that Madame Marcia wasn't alone last night.'

'I get that impression too.'

'Have you seen a man leave the apartment today?'

'No. He's probably still up there. According to the maid, we can expect he'll move in soon.'

'Which of them was the maid closer to?'

'Monsieur Maurice, I'd say.'

'Thank you.'

Maigret and Janvier went up to the second floor. Maigret rang the bell. Several minutes passed before anyone answered.

'Madame Marcia, please.'

'I'm not sure if she'll be able to see you. Come in, though . . .'

She showed them into the large drawing room, which was looking back to normal.

'We'll have to come back with furniture experts,' Maigret murmured as they waited.

When a figure finally appeared in the doorway, it was Manuel Mori rather than Line.

'You again!' he said.

'I asked for Line Marcia.'

'She doesn't want to see you, and I'm going to make sure you don't bother her.'

'But I'm going to bother you both. You are under arrest . . .'

'Ah yes, the famous warrant.'

'There's a new one this time, in the name of Line Marcia, née Polin.'

'You dared . . .'

'I dared, and I'd advise you not to try anything obstructive. It could have very serious consequences for you.'

Manuel made as if to reach for his pocket, in which the outline of a revolver was visible. Maigret said softly:

'Hands away, son.'

Line's lover was pale.

'You'd better keep him covered, Janvier.'

He looked around for a bell and found one near the massive fireplace. He pressed it. Moments later the maid stopped, dumbfounded, in the drawing-room doorway.

'Go and get Madame Marcia for me. Tell her to pack some clothes, underwear and toiletries, enough for a few days.'

The maid had barely gone before the lady of the house appeared empty-handed.

'What does this . . .'

She stopped when she saw Janvier holding his gun.

'Here's a warrant in your name. I've come to arrest you both.'

'But it's nothing to do with me!'

'At the very least you witnessed the murder and tried to cover up for the guilty party. That's called being an accessory.'

'If a wife is liable, every time she has a lover . . .'

'Not all lovers open fire on the husband. Go and get a few things . . . Wait a minute . . . Give me your gun, Manuel.'

Mori hesitated. A hard look came over his face. Maigret stared him straight in the eye, ready for anything.

Finally a hand held out the gun to him.

'Stay with him, Janvier. I don't like letting the wife go off on her own. I'm not sure I'd see her again.'

'I have to change.'

'You won't be the first woman I've seen do that. What did you wear when you danced at the Tabarin?'

The atmosphere was oppressive, and a sense of threat still hung in the air. Maigret followed Line to the end of the corridor, where she went into a yellow and dove-grey bedroom with Louis XVI furniture. The bed was unmade. On a little table there was a bottle of whisky and two half-full glasses.

He thought her capable of anything, even grabbing the bottle and smashing it on his head.

He poured her a large measure of alcohol and put the bottle out of her reach.

'Don't you want any?'

'No. Get ready.'

'How long do you think we'll be gone for? Or maybe I should say: I'll be gone for.'

'That will depend.'

'On whom?'

'You and the examining magistrate.'

'What made you suddenly decide to arrest us when there was no question of it yesterday?'

'Let's say that we've made some significant discoveries in the meantime.'

'You definitely haven't found the gun that killed my husband.'

'You know very well it's in the Seine, like the blood-stained rug.'

'Which prison are you taking us to?'

'The cells in the basement of the Palais de Justice first of all.'

'Isn't that where they put prostitutes?'

'Sometimes, yes.'

'And you have the nerve . . .'

Maigret pointed to the bed.

'You didn't even let that get cold.'

'You are a terrible person.'

'At the moment I am, yes. Hurry up.'

In a flash she stepped out of her clothes, as an act of defiance, it seemed.

'I want to have a shower. There can't be any of those where I'm going.'

She had a beautiful, supple dancer's body, but Maigret didn't feel a flicker of excitement.

'I'll give you five minutes.'

He went and stood in the doorway of the bathroom, which had another door.

It took her almost quarter of an hour to get ready. She was wearing the same black suit and white hat as the day before. She had stuffed some underwear and toiletries in an overnight bag.

'I'm coming with you because I don't have a choice. I hope you'll pay dearly for this.'

They rejoined the two men in the drawing room. It was obvious from the look of surprise on Manuel's face that he was wondering why his mistress had kept them waiting so long. Did he think her capable of anything too?

'The handcuffs, Janvier.'

'Are you going to put me in handcuffs?' asked Manuel, who had turned white and was already raising his fist.

He was much stronger than Janvier, but a concerted stare from Maigret made him lower his fist, and the handcuffs snapped shut on his wrists.

'I hope you're not going to put them on her too?'

'Only if I have to.'

The maid came and opened the front door for them, a strange smile on her face.

'Down you go.'

Maigret ushered Mori into the back of the car and got in beside him, while the young woman sat in the front next to Janvier. Neither of them tried to make a run for it, not that they would have succeeded.

'What about my brother?'

'He should already be at headquarters. Unless they had trouble getting hold of him.'

'Did you send your men to Rue du Caire?'

'Yes.'

'He'd have been there. My brother's got nothing to do with this. I didn't even see him that night . . .'

'You're lying.'

'You'll have to prove otherwise.'

The car drove into the courtyard, and all four of them climbed the stairs.

'In my office, Janvier.'

The window was still open. The storm felt close now, and you could have sworn that it was already raining over Montparnasse.

'Sit down, both of you. Janvier, go and see if Lucas and Lapointe are back.'

The inspector returned moments later.

'He's next door, under guard.'

'Bring him in.'

Jo was as furious as his elder brother.

'I'm making a complaint.'

'Fine. Tell the examining magistrate.'

'How long are you planning to keep us here?'

'That will depend on the jury. One of you could get twenty years or more. You're going to have to do a few years, whatever happens.'

'I didn't do anything.'

'I know you didn't fire the gun but I also know that when your brother rang you in the middle of the night you helped him carry Marcia's body downstairs, put it in your car and go off and dump it in Avenue Junot.'

'That's not true.'

'Janvier! Bring in the person waiting . . .'

'If it's him . . .'

'That's exactly who it is. Come in, Justin . . . Have a seat.'

Janvier remained standing, as if he was watching them, while Lapointe, who was sitting at the end of the desk, got ready to take the interrogation down in shorthand.

'Do you call that a witness?' snarled Manuel, angrier than ever. 'You can buy him for a hundred francs and get him to say whatever you want.'

Pretending not to hear, Maigret turned to Line.

'Will you tell me, madame, whether on Monday night you were in an apartment belonging to Manuel Mori, who you see here, on Square La Bruyère.'

'That's none of your business.'

'Does this mean you've decided not to answer any questions?'

'Depends on the questions.'

Her lover looked at her, frowning.

'You do admit you're this man's lover, though, don't you?'

'I'll be with whoever I like. As far as I know there's no article in the Code Napoléon against that.'

'Where did you spend last night?'

'At home.'

'Who with?'

Same answer.

'Did you know that your lover had a loaded gun in or on his bedside table?'

No answer.

'I'll press you on this if I may, for your own sake, because it is very important – especially for you . . . When your husband rang the bell, you were naked in bed. Manuel put on a dressing gown to go and open the door, but didn't take his pistol with him. Your husband was holding a gun. He headed straight for the bedroom and pulled back the sheet . . . Who knows what names he called you . . . Then he turned to Manuel. Manuel went over to the bed and moments later he had a pistol in his hand. He fired first . . .

'That's the first version. When we do the reconstruction, which we will soon, we'll see if it stands up.

'But there's another, equally plausible hypothesis. You knew where the gun was. Your husband was about to shoot your lover, and you fired first. What do you say to that?'

'I say it's completely mad. I would have had to be there for a start. And then . . .'

Ignoring her, Maigret turned to Manuel.

'What about you, what do you have to say to that?'

Grim-faced, the older Mori brother was silent for a while, then shook his head.

'I don't have anything to say about it.'

'Aren't you going to refute this theory?'

'For the second time, I have nothing to say.'

'So you're just going to leave me in the lurch, are you? Well, sweetheart, we'll see how much time that buys you . . .'

'You'll notice that I didn't say anything.'

'You could have denied it, couldn't you?'

'Maybe I'll talk later in front of the examining magistrate, when my lawyer's here.'

'And, in the meantime, I take the blame. Listen, inspector . . .'

She marched furiously up to Maigret's desk and started to speak, gesticulating wildly. She was no longer the elegant Line Marcia, but a wild creature off the leash.

7.

'It's true I was at Square La Bruyère. There's no point denying it, because the concierge saw us, blind drunk as he was, and Manuel was never going to be able to buy him for long with a bottle of cognac. My fingerprints are probably all over the place too, traces of face powder or face cream, things like that, I don't know . . .

'Three years it's been going on, with me going there at least twice a week.

'And that little thug, that perverted little runt there in the corner must have known.

'As for Manuel – well, Manuel knew exactly what he was doing when he became my lover. He didn't want me, he wanted to take over from my husband.'

She was incandescent with rage, talking in staccato bursts.

'When Maurice took him under his wing, he was just a second-rate little pimp. What you don't know, I guarantee, is that Maurice was the real boss . . .'

Maigret took little puffs on his pipe, careful not to interrupt the torrent of words. Line was swept along by passion, or rather fear. Now and again she turned to Manuel and gave him a look of hatred.

A few hours ago, they had been lovers and accomplices.

Now it was a race to see who could pin the blame on the other.

'Janvier, take off his handcuffs.'

'At last! Just what I was thinking . . . I'd have a job escaping from here, I imagine.'

Manuel's arrogance had just given way to sneering.

The Flea sat motionless in his chair in the corner of the room furthest from the Mori brothers. He still had a terrified expression on his face, and, even if Manuel was temporarily disconcerted, he still looked at him with dread.

He had been afraid of Manuel and thought of him as a sort of superman for so long, he couldn't shake it off.

'I'll come clean, as they say,' she went on. 'We were in bed. The bell rang . . .'

'Were you expecting it to?'

She hesitated for a moment.

'No. Why would I have thought my husband would appear that night of all nights?'

'Didn't he know about your affair, this powerful figure who knew everything that went on in Pigalle?'

'Why would he have waited three years? If he knew, he was playing a clever game because he was insanely jealous.'

'Did you have the feeling Manuel was expecting this visit?'

Her silence was longer this time.

'Honestly, I don't know . . . He got up and put on his dressing gown, which was lying on the back of an armchair. Then he took his pistol out of the bedside table drawer and put it in his pocket . . .'

'She's lying, inspector. My dressing gown is made of

149

thin silk. You would be able to see a gun. Listen: I said I wouldn't talk unless my lawyer was present, and I meant it. But I'd advise you to be wary of everything this woman tells you and make sure you check it.

'There is one thing I can clear up now, though. She was the one who threw herself at me when I started going around with Maurice. She kept saying that he was an old man, that he was washed up. An old freak, that was her expression . . .'

'It was the other way around, he was the one who . . .'

It was Manuel's turn to stand up.

'Stay in your seat.'

An impartial observer might almost have found the scene comical. Enthroned in his chair with a row of pipes in front of him, Maigret was as expressionless as a wax figure in the Musée Grevin. He looked at each member of the couple in turn, gauging their reactions.

The Flea was still trembling in his corner, as if he was in imminent danger.

The younger of the two brothers was listening in silence. For the moment, the Marcia case had been over-shadowed by a bitter, merciless lovers' quarrel.

' "You can take over from him any day you like." '

'That's what she said . . . She's ambitious, greedy . . . She started right at the bottom, because she was on the game on Place Pigalle before working at the Tabarin.'

There was something nauseating about it all, and poor Lapointe tried to hide his indignation as he took notes.

'Had she already thought of killing him?' Maigret asked

in a quiet voice, as if it was the most natural question in the world.

'At any rate, it occurred to her in the first few months.'

'Did you talk her out of it?'

'It's a lie, inspector. The only reason he became my lover was to step into my husband's shoes one day.'

'Once again, didn't your husband suspect anything?'

'He trusted me. Besides it was the first time I'd cheated on him.'

'That's a lie. She's even slept with Freddy, the barman. He can testify to that.'

She swung around again with a look of loathing in her eyes, as if she was going to spit in his face.

'It would be easier, madame, if you sat down.'

'I saw how you eyed up the furniture and pictures at Rue Ballu. I was sure you'd understood and that you were going to have them valued. They were bound to find out the truth . . . But it wasn't this sponger's idea.'

Now Manuel was a sponger!

'The chateau gang, as it was called, was my husband's idea, and he was the one who organized it. He had six or seven trusted men dotted all over France. He'd contact them when he was planning a job, and they'd assemble at the meeting place he gave them.

'The Mori brothers would be there with their lorry and some crates to allay suspicion.'

'What happened to the furniture and different works of art after Maurice and Manuel had taken their share?'

'They went back to the country, to crooked antique dealers . . . I dare you to say that isn't true!'

'It's the only true thing she's said since we've been here, inspector. I can't deny it because the furniture will be valued.'

'You directed operations, though.'

'On the ground, yes. But the orders came from Maurice. He didn't take any risks. In his restaurant he played the part of the reformed criminal, and examining magistrates would shake him by the hand.'

'Was it a good business?'

'A goldmine.'

'That you tried to take over.'

'It was her idea.'

'Are you sure of that?'

'It's my word against hers. You can think what you like. I'm sorry I threw the gun into the Seine, because you would have found her fingerprints on it, not mine.'

'Don't you see he's telling a barefaced lie?'

Just when they were least expecting it, Maigret looked at the Flea, who turned white.

'What time did you ring up?'

8.

'Just before midnight,' he stammered.

'What did you tell him?'

'The truth.'

'What truth?'

'That his wife and Manuel were in the apartment.'

'What made you do that?'

Justin turned his head away almost sulkily, like a school-boy who's been caught doing something wrong.

'Answer.'

'I don't know. I wanted revenge.'

'What for?'

'Everything. I tried to join the gang two years ago. I knew how they worked; I know almost everything that goes on in Pigalle and on the Butte. I asked Manuel Mori to take me on, but he said he didn't need a little runt like me.'

It was Manuel's turn to say:

'He's lying.'

Maigret was chain-smoking his pipes, and the air was blue with smoke.

'You can smoke too,' he said.

'What about me?' asked Line.

'You can too.'

'I don't have any cigarettes and I don't want one from that scum.'

Maigret handed her a packet, which he took out of his drawer, but drew the line at lighting her cigarette. Her hands were shaking so much she had trouble doing so and needed three matches.

'What's your version of the truth, Manuel?'

'He never came to me about anything, and I only knew him from running into him occasionally on the streets of Montmartre. Everyone knew he was an informer.'

'It's not true.'

'One at a time. Go ahead, Justin.'

'I rang up to get my revenge for this man's contempt.'

'Where did you ring from?'

'From the nearest telephone box. I could see the lights of the restaurant in the distance.'

'Did you know all hell was going to break loose?'

'I wasn't certain.'

'But you didn't mind that possibility?'

'No.'

'If someone else had been involved, would you have done the same thing?'

This question threw him a little. He had to think.

'I don't know,' he admitted.

'Weren't you getting revenge for your height and your appearance, which made people stare at you in the street?'

'I don't know,' he repeated.

'Listen carefully to the question I'm going to ask you. You've just told a lie because you're afraid of Manuel.'

The midget panicked again, as if the Mori brothers were all-powerful even here.

'I told the truth.'

'No. The truth is that you were paid to make that telephone call at a particular time.'

'Who's supposed to have paid me?'

'Manuel, of course.'

'Come on!' the latter exclaimed. 'I'd like to know why I'd arrange to be caught in the act by my mistress's husband . . .'

Justin finally started talking.

'He gave me a thousand francs. He threatened to have me killed if I was stupid enough to say anything. He said: "I've got men everywhere who'll do it if I can't." I felt sorry for Monsieur Maurice, I liked him . . .'

'But you still did as you were told.'

'I didn't want to be shot.'

'Didn't you think that Monsieur Maurice might shoot first?'

'The minute that man . . .'

He pointed to Manuel.

'The minute that man decided what was going to happen, there was no escaping it. He's a sort of devil.'

Maigret couldn't help but smile as Line took centre stage again.

'You see, I wasn't lying, inspector. I didn't know about this telephone call, I wasn't expecting my husband to burst in, and so I didn't have a gun.'

'That's not true! Lying comes to her as easily as breathing. The telephone call was her idea. I can still hear her saying to me: "If you kill him or have him killed, doesn't matter where, you'll end up being the prime suspect because the police will soon find out about our relationship.

But suppose he catches us in flagrante, so to speak . . . I know him. He won't come unarmed. He'll threaten you, or maybe me. Either way it's self-defence . . ."'

'That doesn't prove that you didn't fire the gun,' she said, tears of rage in her eyes. Turning to Maigret, she pleaded, 'What do I have to do for you to believe me?'

'It's not up to me to believe you. As I've already said, it's the jury that will decide.'

'I've never touched a gun in my life . . .'

'That's not true,' Manuel put in. 'I saw her shooting seagulls in Bandol.'

'With a pistol?'

'Her husband's.'

'Did she hit any?'

'She killed some while I was watching.'

'Justin . . .'

'Yes, inspector.'

'When did Manuel tell you about the telephone call, and where were you?'

'It was the night of the murder, in Rue Pigalle. I'd just taken Blanche to the Canary. I go there every day at the same time.'

'Did he tell you to call around midnight?'

'Yes.'

'You see!' cried Line. 'I didn't even know where the Flea was, and Manuel made sure not to mention the telephone call.'

Maigret was thirsty. He would have given a great deal to have some beer sent up, but then he would have had to order for everybody.

He had achieved something important, the main thing, in fact. Now they had turned against each other, the two lovers had stopped denying that Monsieur Maurice had been murdered in the apartment on Square La Bruyère.

Their respective guilt didn't concern him so much. It wasn't only the gunshot that mattered, it was also what had happened before, the preparation.

He turned to Manuel, who was smoking a cigarette, a defiant look on his face.

'Why, after engineering this crime of passion, did you call your brother to help you take the body to Avenue Junot?'

'Exactly, that's what proves I didn't fire the gun. If I had, I would have admitted it, because it would have been self-defence. But, the minute Line did it, it became harder to convince anyone of that. I told her to go home and promised her I'd take care of everything.'

Maigret looked from one lover to the other. They were each as capable of lying as the other. Mori was a hardened cynic, who hadn't been stopped by anything so far. But was Line any more sincere than him?

A croaky voice came from the Flea's corner.

'It was him!' said the voice.

'Did you see him?'

'I heard it.'

'Where were you?'

'I had followed Monsieur Maurice up to the fourth floor. I was hiding on the landing. Suddenly I heard the woman's voice screaming:

'"Shoot, come on! Can't you see he's going to kill me . . ."'

'She hadn't finished before I heard a shot. I ran downstairs.'

There was a silence. The Flea's huge mouth had broken into a strange smile.

Manuel spoke first.

'He's lying. Maurice didn't try to shoot her . . .'

'He's making it up,' said Line. 'No one said a word . . .'

Maigret stood up, looked balefully at them all in turn.

'Has anyone got anything else to say?'

'No!' grunted Manuel.

'I'll say it again, he's lying,' Line said clearly.

'Janvier! Handcuff the three of them.'

'But I didn't have anything to do with it,' protested Jo, the younger Mori.

'Didn't you help your brother get rid of the body?'

'That's not a crime . . .'

'It's called aiding and abetting. Handcuff them.'

'Me too?' squealed Line as if she were about to throw a fit.

'You too.'

Then Maigret told Lapointe:

'Help Janvier take them to the cells.'

He was tired. He wanted to think about something else. He put his hat on and went down the great staircase.

Large drops of rain were starting to fall, making black circles on the pavement.

He reached Place Dauphine, where two of his colleagues were drinking pastis. He was tempted for a moment, then thought better of it.

'The biggest glass of beer you've got,' he said to the bar owner.

9.

The bench to the left of Examining Magistrate Bouteille's door was almost constantly occupied for three months. The Mori brothers' – and Monsieur Maurice's – accomplices in the chateau and country-estate robberies had had to be tracked down to various provincial towns.

Art experts had worked away too, eventually discovering the owners of the furniture and paintings in Rue Ballu and Square La Bruyère.

Valuables stolen by the gang were also found in disreputable antique dealers across the country.

Maigret made a special trip to Montmartre to congratulate the modest Inspector Louis.

'I was just doing my job,' the latter muttered, blushing.

'You can join my squad whenever you like.'

The Widower couldn't believe it. He may also have felt torn between his desire to join headquarters and his affection for Pigalle.

The case went to court in November. The chateaus case had been separated from it and would be heard later.

In the witness-box, Line and Manuel constantly tried to blame each other for the murder. The telephone call to the victim implied premeditation and the maximum penalty.

Despite his patience, Examining Magistrate Bouteille couldn't decide between the two lovers who were now deadly enemies.

When Line testified, a voice could be heard in the dock:

'She's lying!'

'Be quiet.'

'I'm telling you she's lying.'

'And I'm ordering you to be quiet.'

The same scene was repeated when Manuel was on the stand.

The jury didn't settle the question. It sentenced Manuel and Line to twenty years apiece, and Jo to five.

As they left the court, all three of them glanced at each other hatefully.

Meanwhile, the Flea had started calling Inspector Louis again.

OTHER TITLES IN THE SERIES

MAIGRET AND THE WINE MERCHANT
GEORGES SIMENON

'Maigret had never been comfortable in certain circles, among the wealthy bourgeoisie, where he felt clumsy and awkward . . . Built like a labourer, Oscar Chabut had hauled himself up into this little world through sheer hard work and, to convince himself that he was accepted, he felt the need to sleep with most of the women.'

When a wealthy wine merchant is shot in a Paris street, Maigret must investigate a long list of the ruthless businessman's enemies before he can get to the sad truth of the affair.

OTHER TITLES IN THE SERIES

MAIGRET'S MADWOMAN
GEORGES SIMENON

'He hadn't seen her arrive. She had stopped on the pavement a few steps away from him and was peering into the courtyard of the Police Judiciaire, where the small staff cars were parked.

She ventured as far as the entrance, looked the officer up and down, then turned round and walked away towards the Pont-Neuf.'

When an old lady tells Maigret someone has been moving things in her apartment, she is dismissed as a fantasist – until a shocking event proves otherwise.

Translated by Sîan Reynolds

OTHER TITLES IN THE SERIES

MAIGRET AND THE LONER
GEORGES SIMENON

'People who have been here a long time have been talking about him. This morning, when I was having my coffee and croissants, it was all they were talking about. The old folks, even the middle-aged people, remember him and can't understand how he could have become a tramp. Apparently he was a good-looking man, tall and strong, who had a good trade and made a very decent living. And yet he vanished overnight without saying a word to anyone.'

The death of a homeless man in a condemned building in Les Halles leads Maigret on the trail of the vagrant's mysterious past, and an event that happened years ago in the close-knit community of Montmartre.

Translated by Howard Curtis

Other Titles in the Series

MAIGRET AND MONSIEUR CHARLES
GEORGES SIMENON

'He needed to get out of his office, soak up the atmosphere and discover different worlds with each new investigation. He needed the cafés and bars where he so often ended up waiting, at the counter, drinking a beer or a calvados depending on the circumstances. He needed to do battle patiently in his office with a suspect who refused to talk and sometimes, after hours and hours, he'd obtain a dramatic confession.'

In Simenon's final novel featuring Inspector Maigret, the famous detective reaches a pivotal moment in his career, contemplating his past and future as he delves into the Paris underworld one last time, to investigate the case of a missing lawyer.

Translated by Ros Schwartz

OTHER TITLES IN THE SERIES